What's Cooking

Gail Sattler

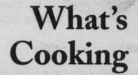

Dedicated to Sandie, my friend and critique bud extraordinaire.

A note from the Author:
I love to hear from my readers! You may correspond with me by writing:

Gail Sattler
Author Relations
PO Box 719
Uhrichsville, OH 44683

ISBN 1-59310-575-4

WHAT'S COOKING

Carolyn's feet skidded to a halt. Her heart pounded.

She wasn't aware that anyone had seen what happened in the kitchen. Obviously, she and Mitchell were not as discreet as she had thought.

Melissa nodded her head. "I know. He said she was his date."

"Mitch? And Miss Rutherford?"

Carolyn heard a chorus of gasps. No one had seen her yet, but Carolyn feared if she moved, it would draw attention to her, and they would know that she had overheard. Her feet remained rooted to the floor.

All the heads stayed bowed in the small circle.

"He told me to call her Carolyn!"

"Get a life, Melissa. She does, like, have a name, you know."

"Yeah, but it feels so strange. She was my homeroom teacher. And now she's dating Ellen's brother."

"How old do you think she is?"

Carolyn watched the girls counting on their fingers and nodding. She wanted to yell out that she was only thirty-three, not ninety-three, and she had every right to date whomever she pleased, but she didn't want to make things worse.

GAIL SATTLER lives in Vancouver, BC (where you don't have to shovel rain) with her husband, three sons, two dogs, five lizards, and countless fish, many of whom have names. She writes Inspirational Romance because she loves happily-ever-afters and believes God has a place in that happy ending. Visit Gail's Web site at www.gailsattler.com.

Books by Gail Sattler

one

"What are you trying to do, poison me?"

Mitchell Farris watched as Jake covered his mouth with his hand, ran across the room, and leaned over the sink. Jake spat, turned the tap on full blast, filled a large glass with water, rinsed his mouth, then spat again.

"Come on, Jake, you're my best friend."

"With friends like you, who needs enemies?" Jake sputtered, standing over the sink with his head bowed, still gasping.

Mitchell tried not to look hurt. "I did my best."

Jake straightened and wiped his mouth with his sleeve. "What was that supposed to be?"

Mitchell skimmed his finger down the page of the cookbook on the counter. "Crab snaps."

All the color drained from Jake's face. "You fed me diseased seafood. I'm going to die of salmonella poisoning, and it will be all your fault!"

"I don't think you can get salmonella from seafood. And it wasn't that bad." At least he hoped it wasn't that bad.

"Did you try it?"

"Well, no. . ."

"Since you're soon going to be my brother-in-law, I'm going to save your life. Don't touch them. And don't give any to the dog, either, unless she has a horrible disease and you want to put her out of her misery."

Mitchell didn't find Jake's comments very amusing.

"Whatever possessed you to try this?" Jake waved his arm to encompass the array of dirty bowls and utensils scattered over every flat surface of the small kitchen.

"Ellen said I couldn't do it."

"Ellen was right."

Mitchell snorted. "Ellen and Mom and I were talking about the rehearsal party and what it's going to cost to have everything catered since Mom can't do very much with her arm in a cast. So I said I would do the cooking."

"We've been roommates for four years, Mitch, and I've seen the extent of your cooking talents. I'm not having hot dogs at my wedding rehearsal."

"I know. That's why I'm making these, uh. . ." Mitchell checked the cookbook one more time. "Crab snaps."

"I changed my mind. Take your life in your hands. Try one." Jake extended his arm toward the soggy blobs, still in neat rows on the cookie sheet. "Sorry, Mitch. I know how you cook. There is no way you can ever make these edible, much less in seven weeks."

"It's too late. I said I'd do it. My personal honor is at stake."

Jake disappeared into the living room and returned with the community newspaper. "If you're really going to insist on doing this, you should take a night class."

"Night school? Me?"

Jake nodded and opened the newspaper about two-thirds of the way through. "Look. Here's one. Creative Cooking for Entertaining. It's an eight-week course, and it starts in an hour. I'll bet you could still make it if you phone right away."

Mitchell glanced up at the clock, then the calendar. The session ended after Jake and Ellen's wedding, but he figured he could learn enough to do what he needed for the rehearsal. He'd made a promise, but he certainly didn't want to poison the wedding party. They were his friends, too.

"I'll do it. What's the number?"

❧

Mitchell arrived at the classroom door with one minute to spare. As he entered, the teacher raised her eyebrows at the sight of him, smiled a polite greeting, and shuffled a piece of paper on the table in front of her.

He scanned the room, looking for an empty chair.

A group of young girls who looked like they'd just gradu-ated from high school filled the back area, about a dozen fortyish ladies filled the rest of the room, and center front, an elderly lady sat primly with her hands folded in her lap.

- There was no one there his own age, and he was the only man present.

The last empty chair was in the very center of the class-room. Trying to act casual, he aimed himself for it and smiled at everyone as those in his path pulled up their knees to allow him access. He slid into the seat. Because he was a head taller than everyone around him, he slouched and leaned back, rested one ankle on the opposite knee, and tried to make himself as comfortable as possible.

The teacher frowned and ran her finger along a paper in front of her. "Excuse me, but I think you're in the wrong class."

Mitchell smiled. "I'm in the right class. I just signed up, and they said I wouldn't appear on your list. My name is Mitchell Farris. Stella at the office told me to tell you she'd fax a new list in the morning. I promise I'll be on it." He waited for a response, but she only stared back at him. "Stella gave me a registration number," he said.

The teacher blushed and scribbled something on the paper. The group of young ladies in the back row giggled.

"That's fine." The teacher checked her watch. "I think it's time we started. My name is Carolyn Rutherford, and I'm the home economics teacher here at Central High. This class is Creative Cooking for Entertaining." She paused for a few seconds and scanned the room, making brief eye contact with everyone except him. "Your original teacher, Edith Ramsey, had to go out of town for urgent family business, so I agreed to take her place. Today, we're going to prepare a few fancy finger foods, favorites at any gathering, casual or formal. We'll start with something basic so I can see the skill levels of everyone here. Let's get started."

Mitchell couldn't believe he was doing this. Jake had rail-roaded him into signing up so fast it hadn't occurred to him that only women would take such a class. And now that he was here, he didn't want to look like a coward and walk out.

The teacher donned her apron, opened her cookbook, and started explaining what she called "basics." She explained to everyone about putting the beaters in the freezer for a few minutes before whipping the cream, but he really didn't need to know why, only that he was supposed to do it. Instead of studying her food processor and all its wonderful features, he studied the teacher.

He guessed Carolyn Rutherford was a bit older than he was, probably in her late twenties. She was a little heavier than most of the women he went out with—not fat, but not skinny, which was probably a good testimony to her cooking skills. He pegged her height at just barely over the five-foot mark, nearly a foot shorter than he was.

She held up some other strange contraption, but instead of looking at the device, he looked at her hands. She had tiny hands, short little fingers, and no rings. Of course, she might have taken them off because she was teaching a cooking class, but he filed the information in the back of his mind.

She wasn't a classic beauty, but she had a cute little nose and pouty, cherub lips with a very attractive smile. Her glasses only seemed to make her face more delicate, and he smiled every time she pushed them up the bridge of her nose with her index finger and kept talking without missing a beat. She spoke slowly enough to be understood, but not so slowly that she seemed to be talking down to her students. Her cheery voice made him wonder what she sounded like when she laughed.

Her fluffy hair framed her face nicely, and even though he couldn't decide what color it was, he liked it. It was a very unique shade of brown—dark, not on the black side, but not red, either. Her eyes were brown, but he wasn't close enough to tell what exact shade.

Since she appeared to be almost finished with her demonstration, Mitchell thought it best to actually pay attention to what she was doing because soon she would be starting to cook. A glint of gold around her neck caught his attention. He squinted and was able to make out a delicate gold cross on a chain around her throat. He wondered if she was a Christian, if she attended church regularly, and how he could find out.

Before he could give it any more thought, she smiled and looked right at him. "And that about covers the basics. Now I'll show you today's creations, which are stuffed mushroom caps and hot tenderloin canapés on pumpernickel with blue cheese."

Before he knew it, she'd mashed a bunch of stuff together in a bowl, whipped it up, and stuffed it into a bag. Next, she squeezed it out in little patterns into the tops of the upside-down mushrooms. He didn't like mushrooms, but it looked so pretty, he thought he just might try one.

Then she mixed up another batch of ingredients, put a plop of the white stuff on a morsel of bread, then stuck a hunk of meat on top of each.

"Now it's your turn. I'll divide you into groups of four, assign each group to a kitchen unit, and you can all do this yourself, following the instruction sheets I've passed out."

Mitchell smiled and stood. This was going to be easy.

❧

Carolyn fought to control a bad case of nerves. Men usually enrolled in the more basic class, Home Economics for Adults, because it was more suited to people with limited kitchen skills. The presence of a man in the more complicated course meant he was an accomplished cook, and rather than simply learning to make decent daily meals, specialty cooking was a personal interest.

She'd already noticed that Mitchell wasn't really paying attention when she ran through her basic spiel prior to her demonstration of their projects for the day.

Carolyn divided everyone into five groups of four, the last team being Sarah, one of the younger ladies; Lorraine, one of the over-forty crowd; the elderly Mrs. Finkleman, who didn't appear to have a first name; and Mitchell Farris.

She directed the last group to the kitchenette in the back and gave everyone a brief explanation of the setup. Before she returned to the first group, she turned to Mitchell. As they made eye contact, he smiled brightly.

Carolyn's breath caught in her throat. One dimple appeared with his lopsided smile, and his green eyes sparkled with humor. His light brown hair, shorter on the sides and gelled on top to hold it in place, set off his straight nose and high-lighted his masculine features, making him more handsome than any man had a right to be. He towered above her, and she estimated his age to be about twenty-seven.

"I'll be back later to check on your progress," she mumbled and hustled away.

Spending time with each group, Carolyn answered questions and made sure everyone took a turn in the preparation of the mushroom filling. By the time she returned to the last group, she had to struggle to quell her nervousness. She expected this group would need little interaction and instruction from her, as Mitchell would be able to help them.

As she joined them, the group was preparing to squeeze the filling into the mushroom caps. Mrs. Finkleman had applied the star-shaped decorating tip and was busily stuffing the mixture into the bag.

Carolyn put on her best teacher smile to hide her jitters. "Why don't we give Mr. Farris the honor of filling the first mushroom cap?"

He flinched, then made direct eye contact. "Please call me Mitchell. Mr. Farris is my father."

His gorgeous smile almost made her knees wobble. Carolyn forced herself to smile. "Mitchell, would you like to do the honors?"

He took the bag and positioned it in the strangest way she had ever seen, with the tip touching the mushroom. Anxious to see his method, she leaned closer.

When he gave it a small squeeze, nothing came out, so

Carolyn had to assume he was testing the viscosity of the mixture, which probably wasn't a bad idea. She wished she could have made notes.

He stopped all motion and raised his head, then stared straight into her face. "I'm not very good at this," he mumbled.

His modesty impressed Carolyn. "It's okay," she muttered, smiling in anticipation, waiting. "Take your time. I'm interested in your technique."

With a small shrug of his shoulders, he squeezed the bag of filling once more, but still nothing came out. Carolyn let her smile drop.

Again, he squeezed it a little harder, but still not using sufficient pressure to start the flow through the designing tip. Carolyn wondered if there was something wrong with the filling.

As discreetly as possible, she checked the bowl containing the mixture that had not fit inside the bag. It appeared to be the right consistency and texture, so she focused her attention back to Mitchell as he gave the bag a small shake, then held it farther away from the mushroom.

He squeezed harder, then gave an abrupt sigh when nothing came out. A quick glance told her the other groups were already half through pressing swirls of filling onto the neatly laid mushroom caps.

Mitchell mumbled something under his breath and squeezed again, much harder this time.

A stream of filling spewed out of the bag. Some of it hit the mushroom, propelling it to the end of the baking sheet and over the edge. The errant mushroom cap continued its trajectory and disappeared off the end of the counter. A long trail of filling zigzagged all over the baking sheet and countertop. With the sudden change in the thickness of the center of the bag, Mitchell lost control and fumbled as he tried to catch it, unsuccessfully. It landed on the counter with a plop, splattering the contents from the open end in a three-foot radius, most of which landed on Carolyn's sleeve.

Sarah and Lorraine stood with their eyes wide and mouths gaping while Mrs. Finkleman lowered her head and stared at her feet. Mitchell stood motionless, staring at his hands, which were covered with the gray mixture. He rubbed his thumb and index finger together, feeling the texture of it, shuddered, and then stuck one finger in his mouth to suck it off.

"I told you I wasn't very good at this," he mumbled.

Carolyn hadn't seen even a high school student's attempts meet with such disastrous results. While she had to pay attention to each group, she had spent more time than she should have watching Mitchell's group's progress. He hadn't done anything in the preparation but had watched the women do all the chopping and mixing. At first she thought it was because he'd done it so often he was letting the novices learn. Now she wasn't so sure.

"You've never done this before, have you?" she asked.

A dead silence filled the room; all motion in the groups halted. Mitchell's face turned beet red. "Can you tell?"

She surveyed the mess on the table, as did everyone else in the room. Giggling drifted from the first group, along with a badly masked "shush" and a grunt from someone probably being poked in the ribs.

Carolyn squeezed her eyes shut and slowly opened them, releasing a sigh at the same time as she crossed her arms over her chest. "There's a basic home economics cooking class on Thursday nights. Perhaps you could practice some basic skills there before taking on a more advanced class such as this. I could have you transferred since their first class hasn't started yet."

He shook his head so fast, a lock of hair flopped onto his forehead. "I don't have time for that. I need to learn how to make all these fancy thingies in seven weeks. I'm staying."

She was about to tell him that the basic class included one lesson on entertaining but stopped short. Something in his eyes implored her to let him stay.

Carolyn sighed once again. "Okay, let's clean this up. Accidents happen."

He smiled and mouthed a thank-you, which she didn't want to acknowledge. Instead, she drew everyone's attention to the front, while Mitchell and Sarah dutifully wiped the counter and Lorraine salvaged what filling she could from the cookie sheet and put it back in the bag. Mrs. Finkleman wiped off her shoe, then used a toothpick to dig what she could out of the tiny holes and crevices in the leather.

When Carolyn started the class on their second project, Mitchell stood back to watch instead of assisting with the preparation, and the remainder of the class time progressed without incident.

Everyone cleaned up their work areas and filed out. Mitchell's group was the last to leave, having had the most to clean up. Carolyn said her good-byes to Sarah and Lorraine and Mrs. Finkleman, but the cause of the flying filling lagged behind.

"I can see there's a trick to putting that stuff into the mush-rooms. I was wondering if you could tell me what it is."

"All you have to do is increase the pressure gradually and. . ." She let her voice trail off as Mitchell stepped closer. Had he been anyone else, she would have been fine with his proximity. But for some reason, being in the same room with this man felt much too close for her liking. Not wanting to appear nervous, she didn't move away.

"It's really important that I learn how to do this properly."

"You just need a little practice. All you have to do is follow the instructions on the handout sheets."

"I'm really sorry about the mess." His voice lowered in pitch and volume, and he reached out to swipe something off the bridge of her glasses with his index finger. "By the way, I couldn't help noticing that little cross around your neck. It's very nice," he said as he lowered his hand to his side.

Carolyn caught her breath and stepped back. She wasn't sure what Mitchell meant by his comment, but good-looking men seldom looked at her a second time, if ever there was a first. And even for those who chose to ignore her plain features, once they got to know her better, men often ridiculed her for being "too religious."

If she let her imagination run wild, she could easily fantasize that Mitchell was attempting to make a pass at her. However, since he'd mentioned her gold cross, she figured he was simply doing his research so he could eliminate her from his list quickly, which was fine with her. She'd decided long ago only to date men from her church whom she already knew were Christians. It was less painful that way.

Carolyn gulped, then swallowed hard to clear the lump in her throat. "It was a gift from my grandmother—when I was baptized a few years ago."

His mouth formed into a smile that made Carolyn's heart pound. "That's really sweet. Can I see you before next class?"

Carolyn nodded numbly. "Sure. I'll be here to set up half an hour before the class starts next week."

"I meant before that. Like during the week."

Carolyn could barely speak beyond the tightness in her throat. "Why?"

He shuffled closer, then smiled, but his eyes held no humor. Instead, it was one of those slow, lazy smiles like she'd seen in movies—just before the tall, dark, handsome hero swept the heroine off her feet.

"So we can talk."

"Sorry. I don't think so," she muttered, deciding it was time to rein in her imagination.

"But I'd really like to get to know you better."

The custodian poked his head into the room, sparing Carolyn from needing to elaborate or discuss it further.

"It's time to go. The custodian needs to lock up the building for the night."

Mitchell blinked and stepped back, and his goofy grin disappeared.

Carolyn brushed her hair off her face, straightened her glasses, crossed her arms, and cleared her throat, grateful that he apparently understood her unspoken meaning. "I'll see you in class next Tuesday."

Slowly, he turned and left the room.

Instead of gathering her supplies, Carolyn stared at the open doorway and allowed herself to exhale, not realizing until that moment that she'd been holding her breath. Before she could fully relax, four fingers appeared in the doorway, grasping the doorframe, followed by Mitchell's head. He smiled and winked. "Good night, Carolyn," he said and disappeared.

Carolyn closed her gaping mouth. "Good night, Mr.—Mitchell," she mumbled, but he was already gone.

two

"Good evening, Carolyn."

Carolyn fumbled with the recipe sheets she'd been sorting. "Good evening, Mitchell. You're early."

All week long she'd been torn between wanting him to come to class early and dreading that he actually would. Every day, without fail, he'd invaded her thoughts. She couldn't decide if she should have been flattered by his attention or angry with him for teasing her.

He stepped forward and rested his palms on the demonstration table. "I wanted to get here early to ask if you would go out for coffee and dessert with me after class tonight."

The knife she'd so carefully selected fell from her fingers. "I don't think so."

"I guess you're right. It might be a little late for that, since we both have to get up for work in the morning. How about tomorrow, then? Maybe after dinner we can take in a show."

She stared blankly at him. Flirting she could handle, but she had no intention of being made for a fool. Other than his being hopeless in the kitchen, she didn't know anything about him. Most of all, she wasn't going to go out with a non-Christian. "No, but thank you for the invitation."

He stepped closer, so she pretended to be selecting matching forks.

"Why not? Are you already involved in a relationship?"

She'd been casually dating Hank off and on for a while. She couldn't quite call it a relationship, but Hank went to her church, and he was safe. "I'm seeing someone, if that's what you're asking."

He moved closer. Her hands froze. "Is it serious? Are you engaged?"

The perfectly matched forks dropped into the drawer with a clatter. "That's personal and none of your business."

He moved even closer. Carolyn's breath caught and her heart raced.

"I think it is since I want to get to know you better."

"I'm too old for you."

For a split second, he froze, then blinked. "I don't care how old you are."

"Mitchell, I'm thirty-two years old. What are you, twenty-seven?"

"Twenty-four. But who's counting?"

She looked up at him. Mitchell was more assertive than she was used to, but he was well mannered and charming. He had a delightful sense of humor and was able to recover quickly when caught in a spot, something she always thought revealed a strong character. However, at nearly thirty-three years old, it was time for her to get serious and find someone to settle down with. Soon it would be her birthday, adding another year between them. She always preferred older men, but a nine-year age difference the other way was robbing the cradle.

Carolyn squeezed her eyes shut to clear her thoughts. "I'm sorry, Mitchell, I don't think it's a good idea."

He opened his mouth to speak but shut it quickly at the sound of approaching footsteps in the hall.

Carolyn quickly adjusted her glasses, then greeted her incoming students.

After she welcomed them, she took her place at the front of the classroom and froze. Mitchell sat in the front row, center seat, right next to Mrs. Finkleman. He crossed his arms, smiled, and winked.

Briefly, Carolyn considered canceling the class.

She was barely conscious of what she was doing as she showed the class how to properly lay out decorative meat, cheese, fruit, and vegetable trays. Next, she demonstrated how to make rosette radishes, carrot spirals and curls, then her specialty edible decoration, an onion blossom. Throughout the entire process, Mitchell alternately groaned and joked with both her and the rest of the class, questioning his ability to do the fine detail required. His protests were promptly met with sympathetic comments and encouragement all around.

Carolyn smiled through gritted teeth. Very soon he would have every woman present eating out of his hand. She vowed to be different.

She continued with the second project, cream cheese veggie puffs, and sent everyone to try their hand at carving the raw vegetables and assembling the puffs. This time the pastries would be filled with a spoon, and she was almost positive Mitchell could handle that.

As everyone proceeded to their kitchenettes, she noticed that both Lorraine and Sarah had brought full-sized aprons and Mrs. Finkleman wore her canvas sneakers.

❧

Mitchell dragged his feet all the way back to the mini kitchen in the back of the classroom. Fortunately for him, today's projects looked easier, and he wouldn't make a fool of himself again.

After butchering the vegetables, he welcomed the chance to make the next project. He didn't attempt to cut the onion—after all, he doubted anyone at his sister's wedding would care if he set out onions that looked like flowers. After the mess he made with the carrot curls and radish rosettes, when he was asked if he'd rather chop the vegetables or do the mixing, he picked the mixing, even though he'd never operated an electric mixer before. This time he'd paid more attention to Carolyn's demonstration, so he knew he could do it.

Sarah smiled up at him with stars in her eyes, which bolstered his sagging confidence. He smiled back, then quickly turned away. While she seemed like a nice kid, he didn't want to encourage her. What he really wanted was Carolyn's attention.

Mitchell caught himself grinning as he absently worked the beaters around the bowl. Carolyn's calm manner enchanted him. She hadn't made a big production out of his major disaster last week. Neither had she fawned all over him. She quite plainly expected him to clean up his own mess without embarrassing him about what he had done.

Also, the tiny gold cross Carolyn wore again this week intrigued him, especially after she told him she'd recently been baptized. She hadn't backed down and told him the cross was just a piece of nice jewelry or that it was simply a gift without an explanation. She'd had the guts to tell him in not so many words that she was a Christian.

After thinking about it all week, he realized he hadn't given her any indication of his own status in his relationship with the Lord, so, if he'd read her hint correctly, he couldn't blame her for not so subtly telling him to get lost. He wouldn't go out with a non-Christian, either.

With all that to consider, he'd had the whole week to think and pray about it, and this was one relationship he wanted to pursue.

"Can I add this now?" Sarah asked, holding a small bowl full of finely chopped green onions.

He nodded and made one final circle with the whirring beaters, taking care that he didn't bump the sides of the bowl. He raised the beaters and tilted the mixer to give Sarah room to dump in the onions when an onslaught of white projectiles flew out of the bowl, splattering everything in the near vicinity.

Still holding the bowl of onions, Sarah spread her arms and lowered her chin to look down at the front of her bright blue apron and the sleeves of her red shirt, which were now enhanced by odd-sized white polka dots.

"Oops," Mitchell mumbled as he turned off the mixer.

"What happened here?"

Mitchell cringed. Carolyn had abandoned whatever group she was with and was now standing beside Sarah, taking in not only the mess all over Sarah, but also the smattering of white blobs all over the counter and up the side of the cupboard.

Mitchell swished the electric mixer behind his back and grinned. "Nothing."

Carolyn bent her head forward, closed her eyes, and pinched the bridge of her nose. "You need to turn the mixer off before you lift the beaters out of the bowl. I really think you should switch to the more basic class on Thursday nights, Mitchell."

He shook his head. "No! I'll get the hang of this."

She sighed, which he thought rather endearing. She returned to the front, and Mitchell listened intently as she described how to properly dice the vegetables, which ones to chop finer, and recommended different types of knives and cleavers for the different jobs and techniques.

Mitchell now knew more than ever that he was in over his head. Besides the cutlery he ate with, he only owned one knife, and he didn't know the difference between it and any other. It had never mattered before.

When they were done, each group sampled the others' creations. Everyone else's radish roses and fruit carvings looked nicer than his, but he didn't care. He didn't want to decorate; he only wanted to serve good food and to say he made it himself.

He glanced up at the clock. Time never passed so quickly when he was at work. Yet they had finished their second lesson. Only five lessons remained before Jake and Ellen's wedding rehearsal, and he couldn't see himself being anywhere near ready to serve the kind of food he'd proudly told his family he would make.

Being the tallest in the group, Mitchell volunteered to do what he did best in the kitchen—putting everything away in the cupboards no one else on his team could reach.

Once more, he glanced to the front of the class at Carolyn, at the display table with all her perfect samples. They emphasized how pathetic his creations had turned out. He didn't know what he was going to do, but whatever it was, time was running out and he had to act fast.

≈

In all the time she'd been teaching, Carolyn had never been so relieved to see the end of a class. She dismissed everyone and busied herself with tidying up her work area. Everyone headed for the door except, to her dismay, Mitchell. He approached her, stood directly at the table in front of her, planted his palms firmly on the surface as she worked, and leaned forward, giving her no choice but to stop what she was doing.

"I can't do this," he said, waving his hand over her display of cut fruits and vegetables. "I need remedial help."

"Remedial help?"

"I peel carrots at home, but I certainly don't cut them into these fancy curly things. I really have to learn to do this stuff. Could you give me extra lessons during the week? I'm desperate." He grinned a cute little boyish grin that emphasized his charming dimple.

Carolyn nearly choked. She couldn't imagine why he was so adamant about learning to prepare fancy hors d'oeuvres or finger foods, and especially the delicate procedure of food decorating, when she doubted his ability to cook even a basic meal.

She continued to stare back at him across the table. If he needed help improving his basic cooking skills, it wasn't like she had anything better to do. Except for Wednesday night Bible study meetings, her evenings and social calendar were embarrassingly bare. She often assisted graduating students in acquiring basic cooking and home management skills, but Mitchell wasn't a student. He was a grown man.

She opened her mouth to decline, but before she could get a word out, he pressed his palms together, widened his grin, and opened his eyes even wider. "Puh-leeeeze?" he begged.

Carolyn folded her arms in front of her chest and openly glowered at him. In response, he pressed one palm to the center of his chest, fingers splayed, and batted his long eyelashes.

"Why is this so important to you?"

Mitchell's foolish grin dropped, and he straightened. "I promised my sister and my mother I would cook the food for her wedding rehearsal. Her fiancé is my roommate and best friend, and he doesn't think I can do it. But I can't let Ellen down. This is important to her."

"Oh." Whatever she had expected, this wasn't it.

"You can trust me. I'm a nice guy. I go to church every Sunday and everything. Promise."

Carolyn's breath caught. All week she'd been wondering why he'd really asked about the cross her grandmother gave her. Now she knew. That was, if she read his between-the-lines statement properly.

She cleared her throat, hoping her voice would come out even, and dropped her arms. "All right, I'll help you. I'm free Thursday night."

Mitchell moved his hands back to the tabletop and leaned closer. "And just to let you know, I was serious about taking you out for dinner sometime."

Carolyn gulped. What had she done?

೩ॖ

Carolyn stood in front of Mitchell's door but didn't knock. She wasn't sure she was doing the right thing in agreeing to tutor Mitchell outside of class hours. She'd prayed about it and received no clear direction, so she had to stand by her word. Besides, it wasn't like she was going to date the man. His age aside, so far she couldn't see anything wrong with him, but at the same time, she didn't see anything that made him right for her. If there were any man she would have considered right for herself, it was Hank, and Hank and Mitchell were as different as night and day.

However, she wasn't standing in front of Hank's front door. She was at Mitchell's, and she was not here as a social call. This was business. Or a favor. Or something.

Carolyn gathered her courage, raised her fist, and knocked. A dog barked, quieted, and Mitchell answered almost immediately. Some kind of midsize hairy brown dog stood at his side, indifferently sized her up, yawned, then turned and walked away, allowing her to follow Mitchell down the hall into the kitchen—where the counters were completely bare.

She waved one hand in the air above the empty countertop. "I thought you wanted me to show you how to cook something today. You don't have anything ready."

Mitchell raised his arms, palms up, then let them flop down to his sides. "I told you I needed help. If we went to the supermarket, could you show me what to get?"

Carolyn sighed. She hadn't counted on doing his grocery shopping. She opened her mouth to complain, but rather than watch his theatrics again, she gave in. "Okay," she muttered. "Let's go."

Minutes later, Mitchell pushed the cart as Carolyn selected the ingredients, in addition to some basics she doubted he had. Walking up and down the aisles, Carolyn tried to shake the cascade of mixed emotions as he teased and complained about the items she chose, acting as if they belonged together.

Once they returned to Mitchell's house, she spread everything on the table, ready to begin.

"Okay, where do you keep your bowls?"

"Bowls?"

Carolyn knotted her brows. "We need a bowl like the one we used in class last night."

"I don't have a bowl that big."

Carolyn sighed. "What do you mix things in?"

"Mix things? I put them in the pot."

She rested one hand on her hip and waved the other in the air in a circular motion as she spoke. "I don't mean when you're cooking something, I mean when you're mixing the ingredients. The bowl you use when you make cookies."

He grinned that impish grin she was seeing more and more often, giving Carolyn the feeling she wasn't going to like his answer.

"I buy the kind that comes in a tube. You just slice off pieces and put them in the oven."

"You don't own a mixing bowl. . . ." Her voice trailed off, and she let out a loud, exasperated sigh. "Okay, we'll use the pot. Where's your electric mixer?"

He raised one finger in the air in triumph. "I have one of those!"

Instead of opening a cupboard door, Mitchell left the room,

the door to the garage opened and banged shut, boxes shuffled, and the door opened and closed again.

He returned with a large box, which he placed on the table, then used a knife from the cutlery drawer to slice through the manufacturer's clear tape. He pulled out the protective foam packing, a warranty card and other literature, and finally, a brand-new electric mixer wrapped in a plastic bag.

Carolyn sighed again.

"You sure do sigh a lot."

She ignored his comment. "Why was your mixer in the garage?"

"I bought it after class last week and put it with my tools so I would know where it was when I needed it."

"You've got to be kidding."

This time, it was Mitchell who sighed loudly. "Carolyn, I'm starting from scratch here. I told you that."

She opened her mouth to suck in a deep breath, but after his comment about her sighing, she quickly closed it again and let her breath out slowly through her nose. "Do I dare ask if you own a wooden spoon?"

"Go ahead and ask, but I don't think you're going to like the answer."

Carolyn buried her face in her hands. "Mitchell!" she mumbled through her fingers. "How do you expect to prepare anything if you don't have the proper utensils?"

"I told you, I need—"

"I know, I know. You need—"

"Remedial help," they said in unison.

They stared at each other in silence until Carolyn gave up and reached for the pot. "Okay, we'll do our best with what you've got. But in the meantime, let's make a list of what you should have."

He nodded, and they set to work using whatever she could find to do the best job under the circumstances.

Carolyn guided him through the preparation process, and despite the extra time he took to write notes, things progressed well. His canapés didn't look quite as nice as hers did, and his cheese balls were a little crooked, but Carolyn assured him they would taste just fine.

Carolyn washed the dishes and Mitchell dried, pausing every once in a while to snitch a sample of their creations.

"You know," he mumbled as he licked his fingers, "I should probably have some of those fancy thingies for dessert."

"Fancy thingies?"

"You know. Those chocolate thingies. They have different fillings and that white swirly stuff on top. You know, when you go to the coffee shop and you have coffee and one of those little chocolate thingies with the stuff in the middle."

Thinking he probably meant dessert squares, she nodded.

"Great! Can you show me how to do those, too? I'm going to make Jake eat his words. And I'll have you to thank for it." His charming grin made Carolyn's foolish heart flutter.

"I suppose I can. I have many recipes for chocolate dessert squares."

"No, I want a special one. I can't describe it, but I can show you."

"All right."

She barely had time to dry her hands when Mitchell gently grabbed her arm and pulled her toward the door. "Let's go."

"Wait! Where are we going?"

"We have to go to the coffee shop and buy some. They're only open for another hour. I hope they still have some left."

Carolyn let her mouth gape open. She hadn't expected to go out. She thought he would show her a picture in a cookbook. Then she remembered he said he'd borrowed a cookbook from someone he wouldn't name and he'd given it back.

In silence, she slipped on her jacket and followed him out the door to his car. Before she knew it, they had arrived at the local coffee shop.

As he opened the door, his other hand touched the small of her back and nudged her closer to him so he could lean down and whisper in her ear. "I see some people I know. Don't let them know why you're with me."

Carolyn's heart caught in her throat. She'd used the difference in their ages to discourage him from thinking she would go out with him, but even though this was merely the extension of their cooking lesson, it hurt to know she was now an embarrassment to him. She stiffened her back and accompanied him inside.

"Hey! Mitch!"

Two young men about Mitchell's age waved at them from one of the tables near the door as they entered.

"Gordie! Roland! How are you guys?"

To Carolyn's horror, the two young men rose and approached them.

"Carolyn, I'd like you to meet my friends Gordie and Roland."

Gordie and Roland nodded accordingly, then quickly glanced back and forth between her and Mitchell. In response, Mitchell's arm slid around her back, then slipped to her waist. Numbly, she glanced down at his fingers. He grinned at his friends.

She probably should have felt very flattered that he was trying to make it look like they were on a date, but she knew he was trying to hide the real reason they were together.

His friends grinned back, nodded, and returned to their table.

"They're good guys, but I didn't want their company tonight."

Carolyn refused to look at him, wanting to cherish the moment, even if it was only in her imagination.

Mitchell ordered them each a cup of coffee and two chocolate dessert squares, one wrapped for takeout, claiming he wanted Carolyn to take it home and analyze it. She tried to convince him there was no need, but he insisted.

As she sipped her coffee, she could feel the stares of Mitchell's friends on her back. A tightening of his jaw signified their return. The chairs scraped on the floor as they sat, one on each side of her. Mitchell's jaw tightened even more. He opened his mouth to speak, but Gordie beat him to it.

"You know, Carolyn, this may sound like a line, but I know I've seen you somewhere before."

Not wanting to further embarrass Mitchell, she shrugged her shoulders. "It isn't exactly a large city. I'm sure it's possible."

"I suppose. It'll come to me."

Roland butted in. "Jake and Ellen's wedding is coming up fast."

"Just over a month from now."

"I can hardly wait to see you in a monkey suit, Mitch."

Carolyn wished she could see him in that monkey suit, too. He looked great in his jeans and loose shirt, but nothing made a man more striking than formal wear. Mitchell Farris in a tux would be a sight to behold. Not that she was interested. If she were interested in anyone, it would be Hank, whom she already knew.

The cutest dimple appeared in Mitchell's left cheek when he smiled mischievously at his friend. "You'll be wearing one, too. Now if you'll excuse us?"

At Mitchell's blatant hint, his friends left not only the table but the building, as well.

"Wasn't that a little rude?"

Mitchell shook his head. "Naw, they only came over here to check you out. You'd better get used to it."

Used to it? She didn't intend to be out with Mitchell in public again.

He changed the subject, and before long, he held her spellbound and laughing at his outlandish tales. She enjoyed herself more than she had in years.

"Oops," he mumbled as he checked his watch. "I think they're about to close."

They made pleasant conversation in the car while Carolyn sat holding the box containing the dessert square in her lap.

The garage door opened as they pulled into the driveway, then the garage. Carolyn wondered why he didn't simply drop her off beside her car, which was parked on the street in front of his house.

"Would you like to come in? We can put our feet up and watch some TV."

She shook her head. "I'd better go. I have classes in the morning, and I'm sure you have a job to go to." Carolyn supposed it would have been polite to ask what he did for a living, but she didn't want to encourage him in thinking she wanted to get personally involved.

He nodded, then escorted her through the house and to the front door.

"I feel weird about this, Carolyn. After a date, a woman is supposed to see the man to the door as he goes home. It's so strange to escort you out."

He followed her all the way to her car.

"This wasn't a date, Mitchell. I'm just helping you with your cooking." She unlocked the car door, but before she had a chance to open it, his hands touched her shoulders and turned her around.

"The cooking lesson ended when we left the kitchen. Thanks for coming, Carolyn."

His gentle smile eased any nervousness she may have felt. Even though she didn't know him well, she thought him quite endearing. He made her laugh, and she'd never been so relaxed in a man's presence, either despite his youth or perhaps because of it.

Mitchell's hands remained lightly touching her shoulders, and he continued to watch her in silence. The dim shadow from the boulevard trees kept them out of the direct light of the nearby lamppost, but the light reflected in Mitchell's eyes.

Before she realized his intent, he bent and brushed a gentle kiss to her lips, then backed up, his hands still resting on her shoulders.

A car drove by, drawing to Carolyn's attention that they were standing where his entire neighborhood could see them.

Carolyn felt the heat of her blush in her cheeks, making her very grateful for the darkness. Mitchell, however, showed no signs of chagrin.

His fingers lightly brushed her cheeks. "So," he drawled, "will I see you again tomorrow?"

It took Carolyn a few seconds to realize what he was asking. "Tomorrow is Friday. Surely you have other things to do on a Friday night than cooking lessons." She certainly didn't, but it was by her own choosing.

"Nope. But even if I did, I'd cancel, just to be with you."

With a line like that, she couldn't refuse without appearing churlish. "I guess we can do something tomorrow," she said, then mentally kicked herself for agreeing.

Carolyn hustled into her car, gritted her teeth, and drove away.

three

Mitchell shuffled the bags in his hands and knocked on Carolyn's door. While he waited, he wondered what the inside of her house looked like. He also wondered exactly how welcome he would be. He knew he'd pushed his luck by inviting himself. Yesterday, the cooking lesson was fun, but the time they'd shared at the cafe was better.

The night had gone by so fast, he missed the chance to question her about her faith, now that he'd established she was a Christian. Today, he planned to find out more. He took some comfort in that she'd finally agreed to see him outside of class after he managed to slip into the conversation that he attended church every Sunday, even though no opportunity presented itself to share any more. But she'd responded, and that was a step in the right direction.

For a brief second, Mitchell closed his eyes and prayed about it. He liked Carolyn. She had an easy sense of humor, yet at the same time, she was mature and responsible. Her smile warmed his heart like nothing else. He was even becoming fond of her endearing little sighs when she was exasperated with him. Once he determined they were compatible spiritually, he could see the beginning of a great relationship.

He knocked again, but instead of the door opening to her smiling face, he heard her voice calling him to come in.

He opened the door and entered, ready to reprimand her for leaving the front door unlocked at night, but before he said a word, he skidded to a halt. Across the room, Carolyn stood on a step stool, her back turned to him. She stood on her tiptoes holding a picture up against the wall, balancing it precariously by the bottom of the frame, a hammer poised in the other hand.

"What do you think?" she called over her shoulder. "Is this the right height?"

Immediately, he lowered the bags to the floor and jogged to her, removing the picture from her hands before she dropped it. "What are you doing?"

She sighed loudly as she sank to her flat feet and rested her fists on her hips, still gripping the hammer with one hand. "I'm trying to hang a picture. What does it look like I'm doing?" Even standing on the step stool, she just barely reached eye level with him.

Mitchell stepped forward, standing almost nose-to-nose with her. It would have been the perfect height for a kiss, but not only did they not know each other well enough for such familiarity, she looked too irritated. He sighed back, but she didn't get the hint.

"You're too short for that. I'll hold it up. You stand back and tell me when it's where you want it." When she hopped off the stool, he pushed it aside with his foot, stuck the nail in his mouth, and held the picture on the wall with both hands, awkwardly balancing the hammer at the same time. "Here?" he mumbled around the nail.

When she didn't answer, he peeked over his shoulder. His breath caught at the sight of her. Carolyn stood with her head tilted to one side, one arm over her stomach, and the index finger of her other hand tapping her pouty bottom lip. She looked so cute, he wanted to put everything down and give her a hug.

"A little to the right. There. Higher. Okay."

As she approached, Mitchell handed her the picture while he tapped the wall with his middle finger and listened. "You can't hang it here. There's no stud."

"But that's where it looks the best."

He tapped the wall again. "This isn't a good spot."

She exhaled another of her cute little sighs, crossed her arms, tapped her foot, and said nothing.

"All right, all right," he mumbled. "Do you have an anchor?"

"I'm not parking a ship. I'm only hanging a small picture. Give it to me and I'll do it."

Mitchell sighed back, but she still didn't get the hint, so he pulled the nail out of his mouth and dug the point into the wall to mark the place. Carolyn stood a couple of feet away holding the picture while he readied himself to hammer in the nail. He tapped the nail a few times gently with the hammer, then took a good swing at it.

And hit his finger.

He clenched his teeth together and groaned, tucked the hammer into his armpit, and grasped his aching finger with his other hand. He hunched over and squeezed both hands between his knees.

Behind him, he heard a loud thunk on the hardwood floor and the crack of breaking glass followed by tinkling as the pieces bounced, then settled in jagged shards around their feet.

Mitchell restrained himself from jumping up and down on one foot, while in his mind's eye, he pictured the frame falling on Carolyn's foot or her feet being cut by glass projectiles.

Both spoke in unison.

"Mitchell! Are you—"

"Carolyn! Are you—"

She stood in one spot, staring at him with her mouth open, the frame on the floor, her feet surrounded by broken glass. He supposed if she'd hurt herself, he should be able to tell by now. So far, he was the only one who'd been injured, and it was self-inflicted. He unclenched his knees and lowered the hammer to the floor. "I'll be okay. How about you?"

"Me? I'm fine. You're the one with the injury. Let me see that." She started to take a step toward him.

"No!" he shouted before she could move, and she froze on the spot. Mitchell lowered his voice. "I've got shoes on. You'll cut your feet if you walk in this. Don't move."

Mitchell crunched through the glass, scooped her off her feet, cradling her in his arms, then walked toward what he hoped was the kitchen.

She threw her arms around his neck to hold herself up. "Mitchell! What are you doing?"

"I'm escorting you to safety, milady."

"Really," she grumbled, squirming within his grasp. "I don't think—"

"Hush. I'm being gallant. Indulge me."

Her lips clamped shut. Mitchell didn't think she'd respond well if he laughed at her outrage, so he bit his tongue and continued.

On his way through the living room, he passed a photograph of a colorful sunset over a lake. Inscribed on a plaque embedded in the frame was a verse out of the book of Psalms, about the beauty of the Lord. On the coffee table he saw a Bible, opened and facedown to save the place where she was reading.

Mitchell smiled. The pain he'd suffered was well worth the result of his discovery.

His next goal would be to check out the guy she was dating and find out how serious the relationship was. She had very carefully avoided saying she was going to marry him when Mitchell asked, which gave him the answer he wanted.

He stood in the kitchen, looking around the walls for other hints of her faith. He saw plenty of cows all over the place, but he doubted she was into idol worship.

"You can put me down any time, Mitchell."

"Oops."

Gently, he lowered her feet to the kitchen floor.

She walked away as if he were on fire. "If you'll excuse me for a minute, I'll sweep up the glass, and then we can get started with your cooking lesson."

He followed her and removed the broom and dustpan from her hand. "I'm wearing shoes. I'll do it."

≈

Carolyn watched Mitchell disappear down the hall with the broom in his hand. He didn't fool her. She doubted he was the least bit domestically inclined, so the only reason she could see why he was insisting on sweeping up was that he was trying to impress her. Knowing that, she tried not to be impressed.

She couldn't believe she'd dropped her picture, especially after all the money she paid to have it custom framed. She'd been so scared that Mitchell had seriously hurt himself she hadn't realized she'd dropped it until she heard the bang as it hit the floor.

He soon returned with the dustpan full of broken glass, which he dumped in the garbage.

"Thanks, Mitchell. Now let's start on your cooking lesson."

Mitchell retrieved his shopping bags, dumped the contents on her table, and proudly showed Carolyn his first batch of utensils and kitchen paraphernalia, claiming he wanted to be sure he'd bought the correct things before he removed the packaging. At her approval, he returned the bags to the door, and they were ready to start his next lesson.

Carolyn could barely concentrate. Today Mitchell insisted on doing everything with a minimum of assistance, only asking her when he wasn't sure of what it was he was supposed to do, which wasn't as often as their previous lesson. Normally this wouldn't have bothered her, but every time she showed him something new, he stood too close for her comfort.

When the lesson was completed, Carolyn packaged the food that wasn't eaten, insisting Mitchell take it all home with him. He set the bag on the counter and held the top open as she lowered the full containers inside, but before she was finished, he reached inside and grasped her hands. Slowly, he lifted them out of the bag and rubbed his thumbs on the undersides of her wrists, causing a shiver that made her heart skip a beat, then start up in double time. All she could do was stare up at him, while he continued his gentle massage and smiled down at her.

After a few minutes of silence, he cleared his throat. "Is that blue container the one that has that stuff with that splatty glop on top in it?"

Carolyn tried not to stammer as she spoke. "That stuff is called toast points."

"Yeah. That. So that means the white container has those round things in it, right?"

"Those round things are called pastry cheese balls."

"Yeah, those, too. And where's that list of more stuff you said I should buy? Did you add one of those pastry-mixing contraptions? And don't you do that sighing thing again."

Carolyn clamped her lips shut and yanked her hands back. Her breathing didn't feel normal, and she didn't like it. "The list is in the bag, and yes, I did. Now I think it's time for you to leave."

"First there's something I wanted to talk to you about."

She checked her watch. "It's late. We can talk about it at class on Tuesday."

"But—"

"I think that's best. Let me see you to the door."

She scooped up a bag, prompting him to do the same. She led him to the door, where she handed him the bag she had carried. "Good night, Mitchell."

He shuffled everything into one hand, and instead of leaving, he slowly and gently brushed his fingers across her cheek. Carolyn closed her eyes. The moment was perfect for a goodnight kiss that part of her wanted and part of her didn't.

"Good night, Carolyn." He dropped his hand, picked up the bags of supplies he'd left next to the door, and walked out.

A small sigh escaped as Carolyn watched him go. It was nothing she could put her finger on, but something deep inside of her found Mitchell interesting. However, from their conversation during the food preparation today, she knew more about his family than she knew about him. Other than that his sister was getting married soon, the only thing she knew about him was his age and that he attended church services. In some ways, she would have liked the age spread to be the other way around, but no amount of wishing he were older could make it so. She wished she knew why he wanted to see her so badly—but then decided the answer was obvious.

She was the cooking teacher, and he needed to learn how to cook in a hurry. He was simply being nice to her because she was doing him a favor. In a convoluted sort of way, she found it disappointing but, considering all else, for the best.

She didn't want to like him. Earlier, she thought he'd taken an interest in her favorite Bible verse, which she had on display on her living room wall. If she hadn't been in his arms at the time, she would have liked to talk about it, just to see where he was spiritually. Even though it was a good start, just because he said he attended church on Sundays didn't mean he was a committed Christian.

Not that it mattered. Except for class, she had no intention of seeing him again.

Carolyn shut the door, but instead of walking away, she pressed both palms into it, then leaned her forehead against the cool wood.

She prayed daily for God to send her a Mr. Right, a man who would be about five or six years older than her, educated, well into a successful career, and understand that her career as a teacher was important to her, too. Not that she was getting desperate, but soon she was going to be thirty-three years old, and she was more than ready to settle down. She wanted to fall in love with a man who would love and cherish her as much as she would him.

She needed a mature man who was a strong leader but was flexible and open to God's direction. Carolyn knew she had a tendency to be a bit headstrong, so she needed a mate who wouldn't stand back and let her make all the decisions or carry all the responsibility just because it was easier for him. But at the same time, she didn't want a man with whom every decision would be a battle. She needed a man who was regal and reserved and with the strength of character to stand by her side and be her equal partner in all things.

She didn't know much about Mitchell, but Mitchell was

not that man. Even though she enjoyed her time with him, she doubted Mitchell could be serious about anything. There were more important things in life than simply having fun.

It didn't matter, anyway. She wouldn't see Mitchell until next class, on Tuesday, four days away, which was as it should be.

&

Carolyn flicked off the vacuum cleaner switch and cocked her head to listen.

Sure enough, it was the doorbell she'd heard. Since she wasn't expecting anyone, she had no idea who it could possibly be.

When she checked through the peephole, a gorgeous green eye stared back.

She ran her hands through her hair to straighten it, then opened the door.

"Hello, Mitchell. What are you doing here?"

He held a large, flat package. "I brought you something. Mind if I come in?" He grinned and stepped past her into the house without waiting for her reply.

Carolyn followed him to the couch and waited while he sat and tore away the white tissue paper surrounding whatever was in his hand. As soon as he made a large enough opening, he pulled out the newly framed needlepoint they'd tried to hang last night.

When she couldn't find it, she had assumed Mitchell had put it someplace safe and it would turn up later. It hadn't occurred to her that he'd taken it home last night, along with everything else.

He held it up for her to see. A shiny new piece of glass protected her work.

Her hands flew to her cheeks. "Oh, Mitchell! You shouldn't have!"

He grinned and, without comment, walked to the wall where the nail poked out, barely staying in place. "Where's the hammer?"

Still trying to let what he'd done sink in, Carolyn ran to the kitchen and grabbed her hammer off the pantry shelf. She nearly dropped it when she turned around to see Mitchell standing in the doorway.

"You keep your hammer in the kitchen?"

"So? You keep your electric mixer in the garage."

He laughed. "Touché." He removed the hammer from her hands and returned to the living room, proceeded to bang in some kind of plastic doodad, then tapped the nail into the center of it without mishap. This time he'd left the frame on the floor, leaning against the wall. When the nail was securely in place, he balanced and leveled the picture, then stood beside her to admire it. "That sure is a pretty scene. I think I've been there. It's around Tofino, right? Did you do it yourself?"

"Yes, I did."

The project had taken her nearly a year to complete. She'd had a favorite photograph from her last vacation made into a needlepoint pattern, which she'd worked on diligently. That day had been the first and only time she'd seen a whale in the wild, and she'd managed to get a picture of it at just the right moment. The whale had jumped out of the water and made a big splash upon reentry against the scenic backdrop of a gorgeous bay lined with rocks and trees and seagulls in the misty blue sky overhead. The photograph was beautiful, but adding the texture of needlepoint made it a treasure. Someday, when she married and had children, she would eventually pass her cherished masterpiece on as a family heirloom.

"I don't know what to say."

Mitchell shrugged his shoulders. "It wasn't a big deal. Jake works for a place that makes windows, so I got him to make a piece that fit. He ended up using a piece out of the scrap bin, so all it cost me was a donut." He paused and grinned. "Of course I made him buy the coffee."

"You made him. . ." Her voice trailed off. "You've got to be kidding."

"It was his break."

She opened her mouth, but Mitchell quickly spoke up. "None of that sighing stuff. Just smile pretty and say, 'Thanks, Mitchell.'"

Carolyn pushed her glasses up the bridge of her nose with her finger. He would never know the restraint it took not to make that deep sigh.

Actually, she rather admired him for being so resourceful, but she wasn't going to admit it.

"Thank you, Mitchell."

He smirked. "Good. That's what I wanted to hear."

"I wasn't expecting you today, as you can tell." Carolyn jerked her head over her shoulder to indicate her vacuum cleaner in the middle of the living room, in addition to the dust rag still on the mantel. "I suppose I could think of something we could do as a cooking lesson."

"I'm not here for a cooking lesson."

Carolyn was touched that he would have made the special trip just to deliver her repaired needlepoint frame. In order to be polite, as well as to show her gratitude, she was about to ask him if she could make him a cup of coffee when he reached toward her, picked up one of her hands, then started massaging her wrist with his thumb in the same way he had last night before he left.

Her knees turned to jelly.

"I'm here to take you out for dinner."

"But—"

"And if you say one word about paying, you'll hurt my feelings, and you wouldn't want to do that, would you?"

"Well, I—"

"So lock up and let's get going so we can get a cozy table for two in a nice, dark corner."

"But I—"

"There are a few things I'd like to talk to you about, and none of it will have anything to do with cooking because, Carolyn, this is a date."

Before she could open her mouth to protest, he raised her

hand, lowered his head, and kissed her palm. No man had ever done that before, and she froze at the soft touch of his lips on her skin. Carolyn stood with her mouth hanging open and her heart pounding as he smiled at her. She still couldn't imagine why Mitchell was doing this, but this opened up an opportunity to learn more about him—if she could get her brain to function properly.

Carolyn yanked her hand away and backed up a step. She ran her trembling fingers through her hair and straightened her glasses. "Excuse me. I have to change my T-shirt. I'll be right back."

Carolyn hustled to her bedroom and selected a baggy sweater to go with her jeans, quickly ran a brush through her hair, and returned to the living room, where Mitchell stood gazing at her needlepoint.

When the time came to eat, she would insist on pausing to say grace over their meal. That would tell her how willing he was to show he was a Christian in public.

Still, no matter where he stood in his Christianity, the bottom line was that he wasn't the type of man she saw as a suitable mate. Even though she and Hank didn't have what she could even remotely call a steady relationship, he appeared to be all the things she was looking for in a man. All the things Mitchell was not.

But if she had to have a reason for being with him, she knew Mitchell would make her laugh.

Carolyn sucked in a deep breath for strength. "I'm ready. Let's go."

four

Carolyn found herself sitting much too close to Mitchell, which was exactly what she wanted to avoid. She had nixed his suggestion of a quiet, cozy table for two at a small, intimate restaurant. Instead, they'd left his car at the Park and Ride and took the monorail to the crowded and busy public market.

Because of the Saturday crowd, the last available seats in their car were the sideways benches. As more people crammed themselves in, the seating became tighter and tighter until they were pressed together from knee to shoulder.

Carolyn refused to look at Mitchell. Instead, she watched two small children, heads plastered to the window, enjoying the ride. Mitchell barely had to move his head, and she could feel his breath on her cheek as he spoke directly into her ear.

"Those kids appear to be fascinated with the view."

She didn't know about the kids, but Carolyn didn't often take the monorail, and she found it fascinating.

The children's giggles set off a chord of longing deep inside her. With no marriage prospects in sight, Carolyn was starting to worry she might never have children of her own. She'd spoken with Hank casually a few times about marriage, and even though most men Hank's age were married, Hank had made it clear he wasn't quite ready to settle down. Up until recently she'd been satisfied to wait, but with her birthday coming soon, even though she wasn't going to get married just for the sake of being married, it was another warning that time was not standing still. She was the last of her friends still single, and her biological clock was starting to tick.

When more people exited than entered on the downtown stops, it allowed Carolyn to shuffle a few inches away from

Mitchell until they reached their destination.

Throngs of people packed the aisles of the marketplace, which was a three-story building lined with booths and tables with sellers hawking goods from handmade jewelry to farm-fresh produce and everything else in between. The place looked fascinating, and she knew she could spend hours here.

Carolyn tugged on Mitchell's sleeve to get him to bend down so she could speak to him without raising her voice too much. "I can't believe you suggested this."

He straightened and shrugged his shoulders. "I come here every time I have company from out of town. We make it a day trip and take the monorail because it's so different and there's always neat stuff to see. Since it's Saturday, they'll have some kind of entertainment outside, too. If we'd left earlier, we could have gone to see a movie at the IMAX theater, but we'll only have time to look around here and have something to eat before we have to go home. It would be different if we'd brought my car instead of using the public transport."

Time flew by as they browsed through the tables and booths and stores.

The aroma of strawberries and fragrant fruit teased Carolyn's nose until they walked past the fish market with its pungent odor of fish and clams. As they continued, the strong smell of the raw fish changed to a delectable mixture of fresh-baked bread and cooking meat and spices, then to the heady bouquet of brewing coffee.

Carolyn didn't need to check her watch. Her stomach told her it was suppertime.

They stepped into the crowded food court. Very few tables were empty, but the area was large and people constantly flowed in and out.

"Pick what you want. My treat."

Carolyn glanced from one end of the court to the other. "There. The Greek place."

Mitchell smiled, nodded, and lowered his head to speak softly and still be heard. "A woman after my own heart," he said in her ear, then straightened and guided her through the crowd.

The only table available was in the center of the crowded area. Mitchell lowered the tray to the table, and they removed their plates and plastic cutlery. "Not exactly a quiet table for two, but it will have to do."

With her food in front of her, she hesitated. This was it—the moment of truth. They were out in public, and it was time for her to broach the subject of praying in a crowd.

She opened her mouth, but before she had a chance to speak, Mitchell smiled and folded his hands on the table in front of him. "I hope you don't mind, but I always make sure to give thanks to the Lord before I eat, regardless of where I am or who I'm with, which sometimes can be awkward. Since you're a Christian, that does make things easier. Are you okay with that?"

He smiled again, waiting for her reply, but all Carolyn could do was nod. His words and actions pleased her more than they should have.

She lowered her head and folded her hands in her lap as Mitchell said a short prayer of thanks for their meal and their outing, as well as for a safe trip home.

He spoke without looking up as he pushed a tidbit of meat off the skewer with the plastic fork. "The verse you have on the plaque beneath the photograph on your living room wall made me think, so I'm going to add it to my list of favorites." He popped a French fry into his mouth and smiled.

"Thanks," she mumbled around the food in her mouth. She didn't want to know his favorite verses. The trouble was, she didn't know what she wanted.

Mitchell popped another piece of meat into his mouth. "I love this stuff," he said after swallowing. "I especially love that I didn't have to make it. Even though you seem to enjoy cooking, it still must be nice to have someone else do it sometimes."

She nodded as she pulled a piece from her own skewer. "Yes, it is nice, and you're right. This is too much preparation at the end of a long day to make for one person. I doubt I eat much different than most people, even though I make my living in the kitchen."

Mitchell froze, then laid his fork down. "Hold on a minute. Before we left, I said we weren't going to talk about cooking."

She tried to bite back her grin. "You started it, not me."

"I suppose I did. Sorry."

At his grin, Carolyn stopped chewing. He really was charming in a boyish sort of way, and it was time again to remind herself not to get too involved with him. She still hadn't figured out why they were together. She was too old for him if he wanted a relationship. It wasn't like men usually sought her, because they didn't. She wasn't pretty, and though she wasn't fat, she was by no means slim. She wasn't glamorous or the life of the party type. She was just. . .ordinary.

Mitchell checked his wristwatch as he popped his last bite of food into his mouth. He took a sip of his drink and put his napkin on the table. "We should probably get going. We have a long ride ahead of us, and we shouldn't be home too late. We both have to get up for church in the morning."

Carolyn stood. "I just want to pick up a few things back at the farmers' market, then we can go."

❧

As usual, Mitchell joined Gordie and Roland in the foyer. They swapped stories of the interesting things they'd done all week, then took their seats in the sanctuary.

Instead of continuing to talk until the service started, Mitchell only half-paid attention to the conversation. Jake and Ellen had just entered the sanctuary. They held hands as they walked up the center aisle and separated only long enough to slide into the pew.

In just over a month, his best friend was going to marry his kid sister.

It made Mitchell wonder what it would be like to meet someone with whom he would want to spend the rest of his life.

He wasn't foolish enough to believe in love at first sight, but he sure did like Carolyn. It was sudden, but he wasn't going to let that scare him away. Instead, it intrigued him. In only a few weeks, he already knew she was different from any other woman he'd met—there was something special and right about her, and he wanted to get to know her better. Much better.

The lights dimmed, and the murmur of voices silenced as the worship leader greeted the congregation and invited everyone to stand.

Mitchell turned his attention to the words on the screen, but not before glancing quickly at Jake and Ellen, who were once more holding hands.

Right then, Mitchell knew that was what he wanted. It wasn't to sit with his goofy friends, but to sit quietly and participate in the Sunday worship service with that one special woman with whom he would spend the rest of his life.

He wondered what Carolyn was doing, who she was with, and if she was thinking of him.

❧

At the exact second Carolyn slipped her key into the lock, the phone rang.

She hadn't wanted to invite Hank inside, but with the insistent ringing, she didn't have the time to tell him good-bye without being rude, especially after he'd surprised her and treated her to lunch.

When she ran to catch the phone, Hank followed her inside, closing the door behind him.

"Hello?" she panted into the phone.

"Hi, Carolyn. Did I catch you at a bad time?"

"Mitchell?" Without thinking why, she covered the mouthpiece with her hand and stared at Hank, who was studying her needlepoint on the wall. The one Mitchell had hung yesterday.

The last thing she wanted right now was to talk to Mitchell. All throughout the church service, she couldn't stop thinking of him.

The pastor had read Psalm 50:1 and 2 as the theme of his sermon. The same verse engraved on the plaque. She glanced over and read it silently. "The Mighty One, God, the LORD, speaks and summons the earth from the rising of the sun to the place where it sets. From Zion, perfect in beauty, God shines forth."

Instead of reflecting on God's glory when the pastor read it, she thought of Mitchell's comment about adding the verse to his list of favorites.

Mitchell Farris was dangerous.

"Carolyn? Are you there?"

She fumbled with the phone. "Oops. Sorry. Yes, I'm here. I just got in the door and had to run to answer the phone. I'm a little out of breath."

As if Hank could tell she was looking at him, he turned toward her. "Carolyn? Who is it?"

Mitchell's voice immediately replied. "Who was that? Do you have company?"

"Yes, Hank is over. We went out for lunch after church."

"Oh. Does that mean you have plans for the rest of the afternoon?"

She turned to Hank. He hadn't asked her specifically to do anything, but he hadn't left her at the door when she ran in to catch the phone. But she had the feeling that if she told Mitchell she didn't have plans, he would suddenly show up on her doorstep. The only way to prevent that from happening was to do something with Hank.

"Yes. I think we'll be going out."

"Oh. I was going to ask if you wanted to join me for dinner tonight."

She wanted to tell him she'd just been out for dinner with him the day before, except that she wasn't sure if their trip to the marketplace and fast meal in the food court could be counted as dinner. "Sorry, not tonight."

"Oh."

The disappointment in his voice was almost her undoing. She didn't know if Hank was ever disappointed when she had other plans.

Good manners and guilt at his disappointment made her reply, "Maybe another time. Good-bye, Mitchell."

"I'll be sure to take you up on that. Good-bye, Carolyn."

The way he said her name made her quiver inside, like he was there, standing beside her, talking in her ear, just as he had on the monorail.

Hank's voice behind her nearly made her drop the handset.

"I see you have another picture hanging on your wall."

She struggled to control her trembling hands as she hung up the phone properly. "It's from my last vacation. Have you ever been to Tofino? I love it there."

"No, I'm not into wilderness. That's not a place I would ever go."

Mitchell had been there before. In fact, he'd recognized the bay in the picture. He liked it there, too.

Carolyn squeezed her eyes shut for a second to wipe the thought from her mind, then turned to Hank. "Would you like to do something this afternoon?"

"I was going to invite you to the opening of the new wing at the art gallery."

She stifled her groan, but barely. "The art gallery?"

"Yes. Since you like scenery so much, I'm sure you'll find a few paintings there to your liking."

Carolyn glanced back at the silent phone. It was the art gallery or Mitchell Farris.

She turned and smiled at Hank. "Just let me put on shoes more suited for walking, and I'll be right with you."

"But those shoes look so nice with your dress. And they make you taller."

She almost snapped that she would change into her jeans and painting T-shirt to match her comfortable shoes but kept her control. "All right. Let's go."

five

Carolyn watched Hank as he stood back from what could be loosely described as a sculpture and studied it in silence.

She couldn't tell if Hank liked it or not. Carolyn couldn't tell if she liked it, either, because she couldn't tell what it was supposed to be.

Mitchell would have said it looked like someone had an accident with a welder after a long day at the factory.

Carolyn squeezed her eyes shut. She didn't want to think of what Mitchell would have thought, but she couldn't help it. She was bored out of her mind.

At the market, she'd looked at everything imaginable with Mitchell—handicrafts, fruits and vegetables, jewelry, and items of every possible description. Mitchell had an amusing comment about nearly everything. She'd almost bought a little bunny ornament that had fascinated Mitchell because of its lifelike nose. In the end, she didn't want to buy anything that reminded her of Mitchell.

But now, even the bunny was preferable over the twisted metal that substituted for art.

When she thought she would fall asleep on her feet, Hank surprised her and took her out for dinner at an exquisite restaurant she'd never been to, which she supposed was an elaborate way of making up for the miserable time she'd had at the art gallery. Of course, that wasn't Hank's fault. He meant well, and she appreciated the thought.

She enjoyed Hank's company, as she always did, but when he took her home, she was glad the day was over and she could relax.

She didn't invite Hank in, so he left her with a chaste kiss on the cheek at the door.

The first thing she did was kick her shoes off her aching feet. Carolyn stretched and wiggled her toes, then headed to the kitchen to make a pot of tea. On the way, the flashing light on the answering machine caught her attention.

When she hit the button, Mitchell's low voice greeted her.

"Hi, Carolyn. I see you're still not home yet. I wanted to say that I just got back from the evening service at my church, and I was thinking that it sure would have been nice if you could have been there with me. Bye."

Carolyn stared at the machine long after the beep, not knowing quite what to make of Mitchell's message.

She didn't want to wonder about Mitchell and his life outside of her classroom or how many times a week he participated in church activities. After his sister's wedding, which would be before the last class, she would never see him again.

She refused to let the knowledge cause her any regret. Instead, Carolyn sat in the kitchen with her tea, opened a cookbook, and started looking for chocolate dessert squares.

❧

Carolyn jumped at every little noise in the hallway. As usual, she'd come in early to set up for her class.

"Hi, Carolyn."

The box of rice nearly fell from her hands. "Hello, Mitchell."

He walked straight to her and removed the box from her shaking fingers, then stood much too close. "I missed you on Sunday."

Although she hadn't exactly missed him, she did feel his absence after spending Friday evening and all day Saturday with him. With his odd message on Sunday, she'd expected him to call on Monday, but he hadn't.

She took the box of rice back from him. "You didn't call me yesterday," she mumbled.

"I had to work late yesterday."

"I don't know what it is you do for a living," she stammered.

"I'm a dispatcher for a commercial carrier. Monday is always a busy day, and the other guy phoned in sick on top of it, so it was nuts in there." As he spoke, he reached into his pocket and pulled something out. "I bought this for you. It's not a big deal, but I hope you like it."

Carolyn heard a little tinkle.

"Hold still," he muttered. "Let me do this before anyone walks in. I saw the cow stuff in your kitchen, and when I was in the mall today, I saw this. You can't decorate the high school kitchen with cows, but this little moo-moo can travel with you-you." She craned her neck and watched as Mitchell pinned a brooch of a small cow, complete with a mini cowbell, onto the bib of her apron.

"Thank you, Mitchell. It's so cute. I don't know what to say."

"You said thank you, and that's enough."

She kept her head lowered and studied the little cow. It was something small and rather silly but very much "Mitchell." She ran her fingers over the little black and white cow, tinkled the bell, then looked up at him. "Why are you doing this?"

He smiled and reached to touch her fingers, still resting on the cow in the corner of the bib of her apron. "Why do you think a man buys a gift for a woman?"

She didn't want to think about that. She didn't want his gifts, and she didn't want his attention. It was all wrong. It was flattering when one of her high school students had a crush on her, but those always faded quickly before she had to take steps to deal with it. This, on the other hand, was different. Mitchell was too old to be thought of as merely one of her students, but too young to be taken seriously as a suitor. Not that she could consider Mitchell a suitor, but she didn't know why he was going to so much trouble to get her attention.

Footsteps echoed on the tile floor in the hall, and Mitchell backed up, letting his hand drop to his side. He grinned, then winked. "I can't wait to see what we're going to make today."

Instead of answering, she stood with her mouth open and watched Mitchell walk to the back row and sit without further comment. Last week he had been center front, where she couldn't help being keenly aware of his presence. She had thought he would do the same this time, but as usual, he never did what she expected. Now that she knew the true scope of his cooking skills, he should have been sitting center front to get the most out of the class.

When everyone had arrived, she started the lesson. Every time she moved, the tiny cowbell tinkled, reminding her where it came from. Now she didn't even have to be looking at Mitchell to be reminded of him.

When it came time to go to the kitchenettes, all the ladies smiled and giggled at his efforts. Carolyn didn't think Mitchell meant to be amusing, but she had to give him credit for accepting everyone's teasing about his ineptness in the kitchen with a smile.

By the time the class ended, even though he'd made progress, he still struggled with most of the basic skills.

There was only one solution.

Mitchell Farris needed more remedial help.

❧

Mitchell glanced at the different cow decorations all over Carolyn's kitchen as she paged through one of her many cookbooks. He'd found a message from Carolyn on his answering machine, telling him he still needed more help with his cooking skills. He didn't know what he'd done so wrong this time, but he was glad for the opportunity it gave him to see her again so soon.

"I know I said I wanted the same squares for dessert as the coffee shop's, but if it's going to be hard, I can always pick something else. I think I'm already in over my head."

"They're really not hard to make. I saw a recipe the other day for something similar. I just can't remember which book it's in."

Mitchell plunked his elbows on the table and rested his chin in his palms, then crossed his ankles under the table. "I can take you out for coffee, and we can bring another piece home and use that for a sample."

She flipped another page. "Nice try, but you came here for

help with your cooking. We're not going out. The only time I go out on Wednesday night is to Bible study, which I'm obviously missing tonight. I couldn't live with myself if I skipped Bible study to go out for coffee."

"Yeah. Tonight is my home-group meeting, too. Tell you what. Why don't we do the cooking tomorrow, and we can go to the study meeting together? You've already met Gordie and Roland. Jake will be there, as well as my sister, Ellen."

"I'd rather go to my own," she mumbled under her breath, barely loud enough for him to hear, as she flipped another page.

"You would? Well, okay. That would be nice. I'd love to meet your friends."

She froze with the page in midturn, still sticking up in the air. "Meet my friends?"

Mitchell stood. "Yes, that sounds good. Maybe next week you can come to my study meeting, but for this week, I accept your invitation. That was a great idea."

"But—"

"I parked behind you in the driveway, so we can take my car. You'll just have to give me directions."

"But—"

"And then how about if after it's over, we go out for coffee on the way home, and I'll buy an extra chocolate dessert thingy so you can compare pictures."

"I. . ." Her voice trailed off, a loud sigh escaped, and her whole body sagged.

Mitchell tried to contain his smile.

"All right," she mumbled. "Did you bring your Bible?"

"Nope—left it at home. I hadn't expected this, but it's a nice surprise. I'll just sit beside you so I can peek over your shoulder."

"You can borrow one of mine," she said, then checked her watch. "We should leave now. Let me get the Bibles and my purse."

When they arrived, a hush fell over the room. Mitchell felt all eyes on him as they walked into their host's home.

Carolyn smiled graciously when she introduced him around, and they sat together on the couch until the leader began.

Mitchell enjoyed what the leader had to say, and it gave him a new perspective on the section they read. He wished he had his own Bible with him so he could have made notes.

When the study ended and it was time to mingle, he could tell everyone was trying to figure out his connection to Carolyn and why they were together.

Mitchell wanted to know the answer, too. He knew how he felt about Carolyn and what he wanted their connection to be. His biggest problem was to get her to take him seriously, but he didn't know how to do that—short of getting down on one knee and proposing, and they were nowhere near that stage in their relationship. He wasn't even sure what they had could be called a relationship.

After consuming too much coffee, Mitchell slipped away to use the rest room. He was just around the corner on his way back when he heard Carolyn's voice.

His feet skidded to a halt. He didn't want to eavesdrop, but he also didn't want to embarrass Carolyn by dropping into the middle of the conversation, especially if it was about him. He stayed where he was, out of their sight.

"It sure was a surprise to see you walk in with another man," a female voice said in hushed tones. "What's going on?"

"Going on? Nothing is going on. Mitchell and I are just friends."

Mitchell held his breath for a second. He wanted to be much more than just friends, but he supposed that being "just friends" was better than being "just a student."

The other voice hushed even more. "What about Hank?"

Mitchell heard a shuffle on the carpet, indicating someone else was coming. Not wanting to be caught listening, he stiffened, gathered his courage, and continued walking. The lady with whom Carolyn was talking blushed profusely at the sight of him, causing Carolyn to turn around and acknowledge his return.

Carolyn turned to him. "Are you ready to go?"

His ego made him want to slip his arm around Carolyn's waist to show what kind of friend he wanted to be, but Mitchell didn't think she would take kindly to that. And contrary to Carolyn's words that nothing had changed, everything had changed. Whoever Hank was, he now had competition.

Not long after they'd first met, he'd asked her point-blank if she was going to marry Hank, and all she said was that it wasn't any of his business. Her reaction gave him the impression first that the answer was negative and, most important, that she wasn't in love with Hank.

Now it was his business.

He smiled politely at the woman whose name he couldn't remember. "Thank you for opening your home. You and your husband have been gracious hosts. Please tell him I enjoyed his teaching and I hope to be back again soon."

Before either she or Carolyn could say anything, he hustled Carolyn out the door and to his car.

After they were seated at the coffee shop, Mitchell did his best to make cheerful, meaningless conversation, but he really wanted to bring up the subject of her relationship with Hank. Just when he was despairing of ever getting more information, Gordie and Roland walked in, straight to their table, and sat down.

"Would you care to join us?" he said as sarcastically as he could, not caring that he was being rude.

Gordie ignored him and turned to Carolyn. "You know, I finally figured out where I've seen you before. You're the home economics teacher at Central High. My brother is in your class this year. Steven Reid. Do you know him?"

Carolyn's eyes widened and her face paled. "Yes," she mumbled, "I know him. He's a nice kid."

Mitchell's favorite dessert turned to a lump of cardboard in his mouth. The last thing he needed right now was for Carolyn to be reminded that he and his friends were young enough to have a brother in her high school class.

He kicked Gordie under the table, but Gordie kept talking. "Steven has quite a crush on you, but I guess you know that."

The color in her face changed from a sickly gray to a deep blush. She picked up her coffee cup and stared down into it. "Yes. It's very flattering, but soon Steven will forget about me and focus on one of the girls his own age."

The word *boys* echoed in his head. Mitchell thunked his cup to the table and ran one hand through his hair. "Steven's a lot younger than we are."

"Yeah," Roland said. "I think you started teaching the year we graduated, right?"

Gordie closed one eye and started counting on his fingers. "Yeah. Too bad I didn't take cooking that year."

Mitchell gulped down the last of his coffee. He wanted to leave and get away from his friends, but Carolyn still had coffee and half her dessert to finish. He turned and made glaring eye contact with each of his friends. "Don't you two have someplace else to go?"

Gordie and Roland blinked and stared at Mitchell.

"No. Why?" Gordie asked.

Roland grabbed Gordie's arm and encouraged him to stand. He nodded and smiled again at Carolyn. "We were just on our way out." He gave Gordie a pull to get him moving, then escorted him toward the door.

Mitchell couldn't help hearing them whisper as they walked away.

"What's he doing with the home ec teacher?"

"Gordie, you doofus. No wonder you're still single."

"What do you mean?"

The door closed, ending any further insight into Gordie's love life.

Mitchell quickly turned to Carolyn. He'd thought his worst problem was Hank, but he was wrong. Carolyn wouldn't look at him. She kept playing with a crumb on her plate, not touching the other half of her dessert. He didn't know what to say, so he pushed his mug and plate to the center of the table and stood. "Are you finished?"

She nodded, and they left in silence.

The ride home was short, but he didn't want a cloud hanging over their heads, and he certainly couldn't leave her for the night without saying something.

He walked Carolyn to her door. When she unlocked it, he didn't wait to be invited but quickly stepped inside. She blinked when he closed the door behind him but otherwise didn't speak.

"Carolyn, ignore them. It doesn't matter."

"It does matter. You could have been my student. This is so wrong."

He stepped closer. "That has nothing to do with anything. We're both adults now. I know you feel awkward about it, but it really doesn't matter, and it doesn't affect how I feel about you."

She looked up at him. As she raised her head, her glasses slipped down the bridge of her nose. He shuffled closer still, until he was directly in front of her, and gently pushed her glasses back into place. Instead of letting his hand drop, he cradled her face in his palm. She'd never looked so pretty or so fragile as she did right now. All her doubts showed in her eyes.

He wanted to find a way to tell her that age didn't matter to him; it was Carolyn the person who mattered to him.

She made one of her cute little sighs, but this time, for the first time, he was touching her when she did it. The movement and the feeling of her breath on his hand touched something deep inside him.

He couldn't stop himself. Mitchell rested his other hand on the side of her waist, pulled her closer, lowered his head, and kissed her. She felt small and delicate in his arms, and her lips were soft and gentle. He was lost. What little was left of his heart left him, and he kissed Carolyn the way a man should kiss a woman he was falling in love with.

When they separated, he couldn't take his hand off her cheek, nor could he make his voice work properly. His words came out too low and gravelly, but he was past caring. "Since we didn't have one today, can we have a cooking lesson tomorrow? At my house this time?"

His heart seemed to stop beating in the wait for her reply.

"Yes," she finally whispered.

Mitchell smiled, then slid his index finger down her cheek and off the side of her chin. He backed up a step, making the separation complete. "Great. Tomorrow then. Good night."

He walked away before she could change her mind.

During the drive home, a million thoughts cascaded through his brain, but nothing came together.

Jake and Ellen were in the living room watching television when he walked in. For the first time, he didn't stop to chat. He grunted a greeting and continued into his bedroom without breaking stride, shut the door behind him, threw his clothes on the floor, and climbed into bed.

All he could do was stare up at the ceiling in the dark.

A knock sounded on his door, but it didn't open. Jake's voice drifted through the wood. "Mitch? Are you okay?"

"Yeah. I just need to think," he called back, then rolled over onto his stomach.

The problem was, he didn't know what to think.

Mitchell closed his eyes and buried his face in his pillow. "Lord, what should I do?" he said aloud.

He couldn't deny that Carolyn had many hesitations about going out with him, most of which concerned his age, but there was also her mysterious relationship with Hank.

He could have been angry with Gordie and Roland for making the difference in their ages so obvious, but something else would have happened to bring it up. They'd only sped up the timing of when he had to deal with it. Unfortunately, when he tried to talk to her, he was the only one with anything to say. Mitchell didn't consider that a good sign.

He rolled onto his back and stared at the ceiling again.

Regardless, Carolyn had still kissed him. The experience was everything he thought it would be and more. He closed his eyes, remembering, then stared back at the ceiling.

Whatever happened with that kiss, there was still the major hurdle of Hank between them. He took solace in the fact that Carolyn would never have kissed him if she were truly serious about Hank.

Mitchell rolled over and punched his pillow. Even if she wasn't serious about Hank, the way things were now, she wasn't serious about Mitchell, either.

He couldn't change his age, but in order to compete with an older man, he could work on maturity. He hadn't considered settling down before now because he hadn't met the right woman. But now that he'd met Carolyn, he wanted what Jake and Ellen had. Commitment. Stability. A shared faith.

Love.

He didn't know if it was possible to really fall in love so soon, but the only way to know for sure would be to spend more time with her. Serious, quality time. In order to do that, Carolyn would have to be more receptive to seeing him instead of him forcing invitations where they really weren't wanted.

There was nothing he could do to make her want to see him, but he knew Someone who could give him guidance.

Mitchell closed his eyes and began to pray.

six

Carolyn knocked on Mitchell's door and waited. His dog barked once, then became silent as the door opened.

Another man stood in the doorway, holding Mitchell's dog by the collar. He was about Mitchell's age, but he, too, was a good-looking man. She thought of Gordie and Roland and wondered if Mitchell had any short, ugly friends. Or any that were older.

He smiled. "You must be Carolyn. I'm Jake. Mitchell had to work late. He called a little while ago to say he was on his way home, and he wanted me to ask if you'd mind waiting if you got here first."

"I don't mind at all." She stepped inside and closed the door behind her.

"Great." Jake released the dog, who sniffed up at her, then left.

Now that his hands were free, Carolyn reached forward to shake Jake's hand. "I'm pleased to meet you, Jake. So you're the one getting married. Congratulations. I also want to thank you for replacing the glass in my needlepoint frame."

Jake smiled. "You're welcome. Nice picture, by the way. That means you're the brave soul who's trying to teach Mitch to cook something besides hot dogs. Good luck."

After experiencing firsthand the extent of Mitchell's cooking skills, she perfectly understood Jake's not-so-subtle wisecrack. She grinned to herself, knowing how much Mitchell had improved, but at the same time knowing Mitchell still had a lot to learn in the remaining four short weeks until the big day.

"Does he often have to work late?"

"Actually, yes, he does. His overtime hours are unpredictable because they always involve some crisis that can't be left until the next day. He never gets any advance warning or notice. It just happens." Jake checked his watch. "And speaking of late, I hate to be rude, but I have to take care of something for the wedding, and I'm already late. Would you like to watch television or something? Mitch shouldn't be much longer."

"That's fine; I don't mind."

Jake escorted her to the couch, turned on the television, handed her the remote, then left.

Carolyn started flipping through the channels when Mitchell's dog, who she knew was inaptly named Killer, entered the room. Killer looked at Carolyn, sniffed once in the air, then jumped up on the other end of the couch, curled up, and fell asleep, apparently quite comfortable with her presence.

Carolyn's finger froze on the remote's button while she stared at his sleeping dog, wondering how much longer she would have to wait for Mitchell to come home. She couldn't help being impressed that he was apparently dependable on the job. Still, she didn't know if the reason he had to often work late was because he was so good at what he did that the company depended on him in time of trouble or if he was the junior man and got stuck with all the dirty work no one else wanted.

Before she could think about it any further, the screech of tires sounded in the driveway. She stood just as Mitchell burst through the door.

At the sight of him, her hands flew to her mouth to cover her gasp.

"Don't worry, the blood's not mine. I'm fine." Mitchell was covered in dirt, his hair was streaked with a mixture of blue and orange, and a smear of blood marred the front of his shirt.

"You don't look fine."

He shrugged his shoulders. "One of the guys in the warehouse had an accident, and I had to take him to the ER, then drive him home. He's fine. It's just some heavy bruising and a few stitches. Do you have any idea how to get blood out of upholstery?"

"What about you?"

"I need a shower, but I think I should take care of my car first."

"Are you sure you're okay?"

He ran his fingers through his hair, studied his hand, then rubbed his fingers together. "Except for my hair, I'm fine. It'll probably wash out, but if not, I'll have the most trendy hair color at the wedding, don't you think?"

She blinked and stared at him. Now that the panic was over and she knew he was unhurt, she could look at him more objectively. "What is that? Or should I not ask?"

"It's some kind of dye or pigment used in paints. I don't know if it will come out."

"I think you should wash it right away, just in case. If you'll get me a sponge and a bucket, I'll see what I can do about your car."

While Mitchell was in the shower, Carolyn did the best she could to sop the blood out of the passenger seat. It wasn't a particularly expensive car, but it was sporty and fairly new, and she hated to see the interior spoiled, especially as a result of his helping someone else.

Only a small discoloration remained by the time Mitchell appeared.

He ran his fingers through his wet hair. "I didn't get much of the color out, but I'll need a haircut before the wedding, anyway. How's my car?"

She tossed the sponge into the bucket. "Pretty good. I think if we rent a steam cleaner and buy a good upholstery shampoo, the blood should all come out. It helps to get at something like this right away."

Since she didn't want to sit in the wet seat, they took her car to the supermarket to rent the unit.

"Now that we have a few minutes, can you tell me what happened?"

"The forklift driver tipped over a piece of machinery onto a skid of paint. Ted tried to run out of the way when everything toppled, but he didn't quite make it. I've got a first aid certificate, so I did my best to contain the bleeding and took him to the hospital myself rather than calling for an ambulance, since it wasn't life threatening. The next shift is going to clean up the mess, but tomorrow I have to fill out the accident and worker's compensation forms." He turned to her. "I also have to do an internal investigation on this. I used to drive the forklift before I got promoted to dispatcher. I know from experience that either the forklift driver was being irresponsible or the machinery wasn't packaged properly. It shouldn't have tipped over so easily."

"Does this kind of thing happen often? You had to work late one day last week, too."

"No. It's something different every time. I have to consider it an adventure or else it would drive me crazy. Did I ever tell you about the time one of the trucks got wedged in the underpass in rush hour?"

As they worked to wash the seat, he told her amusing stories of the various disasters that happened in his workplace over the years that sounded funny now, although she doubted they were even the least bit amusing at the time.

Before long, the seat was as good as new. After they returned the steam cleaner, Carolyn pulled into the driveway behind his car and checked her wristwatch.

"I think it's a little late to be starting a cooking lesson."

Mitchell turned his wrist and also checked the time. "I guess. What about tomorrow?"

"Tomorrow is Friday."

"Oops. You're right. But if you don't have other plans, I'd appreciate it if you could come over tomorrow and we'll try again."

Carolyn closed one eye and tilted one corner of her mouth to think. She didn't know if spending so much time with Mitchell was wise, but she'd committed herself to helping him. As his teacher, if he couldn't do as he'd promised, his failure would also be her failure. She also wanted to bring him up to the skill level of the rest of the class—for the sake of her other students.

She grasped the steering wheel with both hands, sighed, and turned to him. "Your house or mine?"

❧

Carolyn knocked on Mitchell's door. As usual, the dog barked once and the door opened.

Carolyn tried not to let her mouth hang open. "Don't you think you're a little overdressed for a cooking lesson?"

One dimple appeared in Mitchell's left cheek along with his lopsided smile. Instead of jeans and a T-shirt, he wore gray dress pants and a neatly pressed white shirt. Leather shoes replaced his worn sneakers, and his hair was meticulously gelled into a very attractive style. Carolyn narrowed her eyes and looked closer. She could still see some of the blue and orange from the day before, but somehow he'd managed to hide most of the damage. Also, unlike any other evening, night school classes included, he had recently shaved.

"I'm really hungry, and I'm tired of eating snacks. I want real food, so I thought maybe we could go out."

Carolyn crossed her arms and tapped her foot. "You don't intend to do any cooking tonight, do you?"

"I do so, but I gotta eat. Don't you believe me?" He splayed his fingers, placed his palm over his heart, and pretended to look wounded.

She wasn't falling for it. "No."

"Well, you're wrong. I just wanted to go somewhere nice, not too fancy, but not the local hamburger joint, and then we'll come home and get down to business. Please?"

Carolyn let out a long, exasperated sigh.

"You're doing that sighing thing again. I thought we could go to the new steakhouse. I've heard good things about it, although I haven't been there yet."

"All right, but you had better be prepared to do some cooking when we get back."

Mitchell reached into the closet and yanked out his jacket, then stepped outside.

He opened the car door and waited for her to get in. "You look nice, by the way."

She wore her comfortable flat shoes and her denim skirt and a fuzzy pink sweater, which would be fine for where they were going; but for once, Mitchell was dressed better than she was. It felt strange. "Thank you. You look nice, too."

Not only did he look good, he smelled good. In the confines of the car, she could smell a spicy aftershave or cologne— something she'd never noticed about him before, which made her suspect that in his mind this was a date. And, contrary to her claims, she had indeed fallen for it.

When they arrived at the restaurant, he was the perfect gentleman.

Combining his new cultivated appearance with his polished manners, he looked and acted older, which was a perverse reminder of how young he really was.

As they talked, in the back of her mind, Carolyn thought of her own life and what she was doing when she was twenty-four years old. That was nine years ago, and she was just beginning her teaching career. So much time had passed, and she'd grown up a lot in those years.

When the waiter returned with their meals, Mitchell closed his eyes and bowed his head to pause for a word of prayer before they ate.

Something in Carolyn's heart went haywire. The young man before her, now dressed in his good clothes, ready to pray in public completely unashamed, was the same man who had given her a silly piece of tinkly cow costume jewelry only days ago.

Cow jewelry.

Hank would have given her diamonds. Diamonds and real gold were in Hank's nature. Mature. Dignified. Conservative.

Carolyn forced herself to stop staring at Mitchell and closed her eyes. Mitchell would never be conservative. It wasn't in him. He wasn't even wearing a tie to go out, which made her suspect that the only ties he owned had cartoon characters on them.

She recalled the three-piece suit with a matching monochrome tie Hank had worn to the last Christmas banquet. Hank was thirty-nine, six years older than she would be on her upcoming birthday. About six months ago, Carolyn had noticed a few gray hairs around Hank's temples and mentioned it to him. The next time she saw him, they were gone.

Carolyn didn't know how Mitchell had hidden most of the blue and orange, but it made her wonder if he would bother trying to hide any gray hairs when the time came. Instead, she suspected Mitchell would flaunt them as a sign of alleged maturity.

When Mitchell started to pray softly, Carolyn closed off her thoughts of Hank, prayed with Mitchell, and concentrated on having a lovely meal with him.

After the plates were cleared, the waiter returned to ask if they wanted dessert.

Mitchell shook his head. "No, thank you. We'll have the bill, please."

When the waiter left, Carolyn turned to Mitchell. "You could have ordered something if you wanted."

"We have to get back. You still have to show me enough so I don't make a fool of myself on Tuesday."

"Pardon me?"

"The cooking lesson? Isn't that why you came over in the first place?"

"You mean you really want to cook tonight?"

"Didn't I say that earlier?"

Carolyn struggled not to raise her hands to cover the heat in her cheeks. "I'm so sorry, Mitchell. I didn't believe you. I don't know what to say."

"This has been a real treat, not to have to grab something at a fast-food place. This isn't the kind of place a guy can go to eat alone. I got to eat a real supper today, and I enjoyed it."

She hadn't thought about what a single man usually ate. "You must eat fast food a lot, don't you?"

His cheeks turned red. Carolyn thought it quite endearing to see a man blush. "Most single guys do, you know."

As soon as they got back to Mitchell's house, he excused himself to change. Within minutes, except for the perfect hair and clean-shaven chin, he was back to the Mitchell she was used to.

Carolyn rolled up her sleeves and showed him how to properly separate eggs and beat the whites until they were just the right consistency. She then made him fold them into the mixture properly, being careful not to stir, resulting in the perfect texture.

"Is all this really necessary?" he grumbled as he spooned the filling into the pastry shells she had shown him how to make because he didn't know how to use a pastry cutter.

"As I recall, you're the one who said he would prepare all the food for the party rather than getting a caterer."

He mumbled something she couldn't make out, and she chose not to ask him to repeat himself.

The baked cuplets were as good as any she could have done herself, and she told him so. She struggled not to laugh as he tried to downplay the pride in his accomplishment.

"And on that note, it's time for me to go home."

"I'll walk you out."

He followed her outside to the driveway.

"It's a gentleman's duty to escort a lady to safety. If I can't escort you home, the best I can do is see you safely to your car."

Carolyn unlocked the car door and stood back before opening it. "This really isn't necessary."

"But it is. I won't be able to see you tomorrow because we have the fittings for the tuxes."

She hadn't intended on seeing him tomorrow, regardless. "But—"

Before she had the chance to move, Mitchell stepped closer and cupped her face in his hands. He leaned down until their noses were almost touching, and his voice dropped to a low whisper. "I'll miss you, Carolyn."

And then he kissed her, softly and gently and so fast that she didn't have a chance to respond. When he backed up, he let his hands drop and opened the car door for her.

His eyes shone in the light of the streetlamp at the end of the driveway as he smiled down at her. In a flash, she slid into the driver's seat and pulled the door shut.

He rested his hands on top of the car and bent over until his face was level with hers. "Good night, Carolyn. Sleep well." Then he stood and walked into the house.

seven

Mitchell wiped his palms on his pants and knocked on Carolyn's door. Her car was in her driveway, but there was a car behind it he didn't recognize. Part of him hoped this was his chance to meet the elusive Hank, and part of him dreaded it.

When Carolyn opened the door to see him, her face turned a ghastly shade of gray. Mitchell looked past her into the living room.

A man wearing an expensive three-piece suit and matching silk tie sat on Carolyn's couch, making Mitchell glad that in his mad rush to get out the door this morning, he had at least grabbed his good pants instead of the usual jeans.

"Mitchell," Carolyn stammered. "What a surprise to see you here. Please come in."

The other man stood.

"Hank, this is Mitchell."

Mitchell noticed the lines around Hank's eyes and the receding hairline.

Warning bells went off in Mitchell's head. Not only was Hank much older than he was, Hank appeared much older than Carolyn. Mitchell's stomach knotted, and he wondered if he might be sick.

Mitchell ran his fingers through his hair, giving the top a slight fluff to emphasize that it was still all his own and it was still all there, then forced himself to smile as he extended one hand. "Very pleased to meet you, Hank," he said, praying for God's forgiveness for the lie.

Hank offered his hand as if he hadn't a care in the world, while Mitchell was ready to break out into a cold sweat.

"Pleased to meet you, too, Mitchell. I hear Carolyn has

been helping with your culinary skills."

He wasn't sure how he felt knowing Carolyn had mentioned him to Hank, but he had a bad feeling that because she had, she didn't see him as Hank's competition. .

"That's right." Mitchell gave Hank's hand a little squeeze, then released it, not breaking eye contact.

Carolyn rested her tiny hand on his arm, distracting him from sizing up Hank. Taking advantage of her attentions, Mitchell covered her hand with his and patted it as she spoke. "Not that it isn't nice to see you, Mitchell, but what are you doing here?"

"I was just in the neighborhood and thought I'd drop in to see if you were busy this afternoon."

"Actually, we're not—"

Hank stepped forward, close enough to Carolyn that she pulled her hand out and stepped back, and when she did, Hank reached behind her and rested his fingertips on the small of her back. "Actually, we were just on our way out. We're going to my nephew's junior golf tournament and then out for dinner afterward."

Carolyn stepped away from Hank's touch. "A golf tournament?" Carolyn turned to Mitchell. "Perhaps you would like to join us?"

Mitchell couldn't think of anything less fun to do. He'd only tried golf once in his life, and he didn't like it, even if he could afford the greens fees.

Hank's voice dropped in pitch and came out rather tight. "I'm sure your student has other things to do, Carolyn. With his friends."

Mitchell glanced quickly at Hank. He was able to ignore Hank's little dig, but he wasn't able to tamp down his triumphant smirk at Hank's indignation to Carolyn's invitation. However, after taking one look at Carolyn, he snapped his mouth shut and held back from commenting. Carolyn was holding her breath, her lips were clamped tight, and she stood as stiff as a board. She hadn't been this tense when she'd caught him using the largest meat cleaver to chop the lettuce in cooking class.

He could only imagine what it would be like for her with the three of them together for the afternoon. From Hank's demeanor, Mitchell anticipated more snide comments, which would make Hank look less than gracious but would put Carolyn in an uncomfortable position.

Mitchell pasted on a phony smile. "I think I'll pass. Have a nice time. If you'll excuse me, I think I should be going."

It was the hardest thing he ever did, but Mitchell said a polite good-bye and went home.

❧

Carolyn adjusted the display mirror above her head. "Can everyone see now?"

When the class members nodded, she continued with her demonstration. Carefully, she pinched the edges of the bite-sized pastry and twirled it to seal it and make the correct shape. She raised her head and smiled at everyone. "There. Now it's your turn. Does anyone have any questions before we break into groups?" She surveyed the room, then pointed to one of the ladies near the front whose arm was raised. "Evelyn?"

The young woman stood to be heard. "Yes, I was wondering if I could do the seal with a fork because I. . ." Evelyn's face paled, her eyes widened, and her gaze lowered, staring at Carolyn's feet. Her hands clenched into fists, and she pressed them to her mouth.

Carolyn lowered her head to see what Evelyn was looking at.

A blur of white streaked across her feet, and Evelyn screeched.

"A raaaaaaaat!"

The entire class erupted into a state of panic. Women screamed. Two ladies ran out the door. Most jumped onto chairs. Those that remained sitting lifted their feet up and scanned the area nervously, clutching their knees with their arms. Mitchell stiffly sat in his chair, his feet on the floor, his arms crossed tightly on his chest. She wondered what was going through his mind but didn't have time to think about it.

"Class! Wait!" Carolyn waved her hands in the air. "Please! Everyone, calm down! They're not rats! They're white mice! They escaped from the biology lab this afternoon. They're quite harmless. Most of them have been captured, but a few are still unaccounted for. Please, everyone sit down!"

Evelyn hunkered down on her chair, keeping her feet above the floor. "It was a rat," she whimpered. "I saw it."

Carolyn feared the poor woman was going to break into tears, but she had to think of the welfare of the class as a whole, not one single member. After a few minutes, order was restored, although no one had their feet on the floor except Mitchell, who was wearing cowboy boots that safely covered his feet and ankles.

Very slowly, he stood. "Is there something I can do?"

Carolyn nodded. "Yes. Would you please go find the custodian? And also we'll need a cage from the biology lab."

He glanced quickly at unit four, where the mouse had gone. "Sure."

"Thank you, Mitchell."

Everyone remained frozen to their seats while Mitchell walked out the door. All was quiet in the room, the only sound being the tap of Mitchell's cowboy boots echoing in the empty hallway and fading in the distance. Knowing that Mitchell had attended high school at Central, she wondered if he felt strange walking down the halls now, years later, at night when the school was relatively empty; but she had never been so glad he was there. He was possibly the only class member who knew where to find both the custodian and the biology lab.

The thought nearly caused her to drop the pastry roller in her hand. Even though she hadn't known him then, he'd been a high school student when she'd become a teacher.

Time stretched as no one moved or spoke. When Carolyn couldn't stand it anymore, she tried to distract the class with a few suggestions on menu planning.

Finally, Mitchell returned, cage in hand. "I couldn't find the custodian anywhere so I left him a note, but I thought I shouldn't wait to bring the cage."

Everyone in the class remained cowering in their chairs; although a few brave souls lowered their feet, they were still jumpy and kept anxiously searching the floor. Carolyn guessed that until the mouse was caught, no one would pay attention to anything else she had to say, much less actually walk across the room to the kitchen units.

She could no longer wait for the custodian to appear.

"Well, Mitchell, it looks like it's up to us to catch the errant rodent."

His face paled. "Us? Like, you and me?"

"We can't let it escape, and I can't continue class until it's caught. I saw it go under the sink in Unit Four."

His voice dropped to a whisper. "Are you sure it's just a mouse? Evelyn said it was a rat."

She walked toward the last known location of the missing mouse with Mitchell following close behind with the cage. "It's a mouse."

"Did you see it? Or are you just assuming it's one of the missing mice."

Both of them dropped to their hands and knees. She heard scurrying inside the closed cupboard under the sink. Mitchell laid the cage on the floor and jerked his hands away.

Carolyn narrowed her eyes. As much as he was trying to hide it, Mitchell's hands were trembling, and he wouldn't go close to the small hole through which the mouse had passed.

She couldn't understand why everyone was afraid of a little mouse. She'd often been in the biology lab to feed them kitchen scraps.

Being careful to be quiet since they were the center of attention, Carolyn lowered her voice to the faintest of whispers so Mitchell would be the only one to hear her. "It really is a mouse. I saw it. What's wrong?"

He spoke so softly she could barely hear. "I was bitten by a rat when I was a kid and had to undergo a series of very painful rabies shots. On top of that, my class had just studied the Black Plague. Even though the doctors insisted I wouldn't, I really thought I was going to die. I'm still skittish about rats—and mice, apparently. I feel like an idiot."

Her heart went out to him for admitting such a thing while they were in the middle of trying to deal with the fugitive mouse. "I don't know what to say. If you'd like to sit down. . ."

"No, if you say it's a mouse, I believe you. Besides, God has not given us a spirit of fear. Let's just catch the little escapist and get on with the class."

Slowly, they opened the cupboard door just wide enough to fit the opening to the cage, using the dustpan underneath to make sure it didn't squeeze through the space. Mitchell held the cage and dustpan in place while Carolyn shooed the little mouse into the cage with the broom. She worried Mitchell was going to faint, but he gritted his teeth and held himself together.

She heard him click the cage door shut, confining their prey. "Got him!" he called out in triumph. "I'll go take him back to the biology lab."

He held the handle of the cage containing the star attraction very carefully, cautious not to let his fingers get too close to the bars. As he stood, the class broke out into boisterous cheers and applause. At the clamor, Mitchell stood still, his eyes wide, and smiled so hesitantly his dimple didn't appear.

Since he wasn't moving, Carolyn sidestepped him and blocked his path. She clasped her hands together and tucked them beside her chin. "Our hero!" she singsonged.

She didn't know what made her do it. Maybe it was because she was so impressed at how he'd handled his obvious fear or maybe it was because Mitchell was already so flustered, but she couldn't help herself. She stood on her tiptoes, gently rested her hands on his shoulders, and gave him a quick and gentle peck on the cheek in front of everyone.

The applause and cheers increased in tempo and volume. Mitchell's face turned beet red, and he left without a word.

Carolyn adjusted her glasses, then turned back to the class, which had finally quieted. "Okay, class, if we hurry, we can still make both projects. Divide into your groups while Mitchell goes to the biology lab, and let's get started."

The whole time Mitchell was gone, she couldn't help thinking of what she'd done. Judging from Mitchell's red face and the speed at which he left the room, she'd embarrassed him more than she had embarrassed herself.

Above all, she couldn't figure out why she'd done such a thing, as impulsiveness was not in her nature. It had only been meant as a joke, but Mitchell might have taken it the wrong way.

⋙

No matter how hard he tried, Mitchell couldn't concentrate on the lesson. He finally managed to push the memory of the rodent's beady little eyes out of his mind; but as if his humiliating admission about his childhood trauma hadn't been bad enough, every time he looked at Carolyn, he remembered her kiss.

Though it was only a quick peck on the cheek, Carolyn had kissed him in front of the class.

For the first time, he allowed himself to be encouraged that she might overcome her anxieties about their developing relationship. She'd responded the one time he'd kissed her properly; but this time she'd initiated it, and most important, she'd done it in front of the entire cooking class.

Unfortunately, the novelty of a man in a cooking class had lost its charm, so the ladies actually expected him to do his share of the work. He did his best to do what was required, but Sarah kept poking him every time Carolyn came near them. He would have done better if he hadn't known Carolyn was watching.

By the time the class was over, it had been the longest night of his life. He deliberately took longer than necessary to clean up so he would be the last person remaining except for Carolyn. He watched as she began to scoop up her bag of supplies, a huge cookbook, and her purse.

He joined her at the demonstration table. "I can carry some of that for you."

"Thanks, but we're going in opposite directions. I'm parked in the staff lot in back."

"I know that. I want to escort you safely to your car. It's dark out there."

She hesitated for a second and then sighed. Otherwise, she didn't protest, so Mitchell picked up the heavier items and walked with her toward the staff exit.

Unfortunately, the missing custodian was now standing in the doorway, awaiting their approach.

"Now he shows up," Mitchell grumbled.

"It's his job to make sure we get to our cars safely and wait until we exit the parking lot."

"Tell him his services are no longer required. It's now my job to be the hero."

She sighed again. Mitchell bit his lower lip to keep from smiling.

"District regulations, Mitchell."

The custodian didn't say anything, but Mitchell thought Mr. O'Sullivan looked at him strangely as he walked past carrying Carolyn's bags.

When they arrived at her car, Carolyn piled everything into his arms while she dug into her purse for her keys.

"See. You needed me after all."

"Yes. Thanks for helping catch the mouse. The whole class appreciated it."

He didn't care about the class. He only cared about Carolyn. He helped her load everything into the backseat, then waited for her to be seated behind the wheel.

"About tomorrow night. I'll pick you up at seven for Bible study." He smiled and closed the door behind her, then turned and walked away before she could respond or turn him down.

All the way home, he continued to think about what he

could do to change the direction of their relationship. He didn't come up with an answer, but one thing he did know. It was time to quit fooling around and be more direct.

Once he climbed into bed, Mitchell closed his eyes, folded his hands over his chest, and lay still. What he wanted wasn't as important as what God wanted.

He opened his heart to God and prayed for a solution.

His eyes shot open. He had to prove his intentions in a concrete way, and nothing stated a man's intentions better than jewelry. Except for earrings and the cross necklace from her grandmother, Carolyn didn't wear jewelry of any kind. He didn't know if that was because she didn't like jewelry or simply that nobody else had given her anything to call special—besides the cow pin, which she had worn to every class since.

There was only one way to find out.

Mitchell smiled and rolled onto his side, pulled the blankets up to his chin, and closed his eyes. This time he would get her something more serious, something to better represent his intentions. Tonight his dreams would involve shopping.

eight

Mitchell managed to get off work on time Friday night. He didn't allow himself to be distracted by stopping for supper first. He headed straight for the mall and the jewelry store.

When he first made his decision to buy something for Carolyn, he hadn't considered how much he would spend; but now that he was in the store, he realized that different items would carry with them a different message. After browsing through everything the store had to offer, he narrowed his choices to either earrings or a ring.

"May I help you?"

He turned toward a middle-aged lady with a bad dye job, wearing a conservative two-piece dress. She smiled at him with a practiced smile as phony as her hair.

"I'm here to buy a gift for someone special."

The woman clasped her hands together. "You've certainly come to the right place. Did you want to look at engagement rings?"

Her question made him aware of where he was standing. He definitely wasn't in a position to buy an engagement ring. Such a commitment was for a courtship that had already withstood the test of time. "Not an engagement ring, no, but something special."

She led him to the next display case filled with rings of every size and color and description. The more he thought about it, the more he thought that a ring would be a good choice. A ring was a classic and tangible way to show how serious he was about courting her properly. If things went well, it might even be a precursor to that engagement ring.

However, most of the rings in the case were too flamboyant, the stones too prominent, or the settings too ornate. Not only did he not like a single one of them, he doubted Carolyn would accept something so large and obviously expensive. Her home was filled with simple things. He suspected every item she displayed held some degree of personal value to her.

"Those are too big. She's got really small hands. I want something delicate and understated. Nothing showy."

He was about to tell the woman that nothing in the case interested him and move on to the case containing the earrings when a selection of smaller rings in the corner caught his eye. In the middle of the grouping was a thin gold ring with a tiny diamond set in a dainty heart shape. Carolyn wasn't the flowers and lace type, but the simple understated message of the small heart was exactly right.

He pointed to it. "May I see that one?"

The woman pulled out the section, plucked the tiny ring from its velvet perch, and gently dropped it into Mitchell's hand. As he held it up, the small diamond twinkled brilliantly in the bright fluorescent light, and the gold reflected both the light above and the gleaming sparkle of the diamond.

"If you're looking for a promise ring, we have a better selection in the other case that I can show you."

"A promise ring?"

"A ring like that is called a promise ring, although often women choose to wear them as pinkie rings."

Mitchell smiled. Then the ring was all the more perfect. "This is exactly what I want."

"And what size will you need?"

He slipped the ring onto his pinkie, trying to picture the size of Carolyn's fingers. The ring barely went past the first joint. "I have no idea. This one is probably close, I guess. Can you size it after I give it to her?"

"Certainly."

Mitchell listened politely to the woman prattle away about promise rings in general as she processed his credit card and rang up the sale. When everything was completed, she tucked the ring into a small blue velvet pouch, dropped it into a store bag, and handed it to him.

Mitchell tucked it into his pocket, patted it, smiled a thank-you, quickly checked the time, and left the store.

Tonight he was going to present his gift to a very special woman.

❧

Carolyn turned off the electric mixer and listened. The door-bell rang again, confirming that she had not lost her mind. She hadn't arranged for Mitchell to have another cooking lesson this evening, and Hank never came without calling first, therefore she suspected that, perhaps because it was a Friday night, Wendy was paying her a surprise visit.

She peeked through the peephole. Instead of Wendy or a striking green eye staring back, she saw the entire owner of that eye.

She opened the door. "Mitchell? I wasn't expecting you."

"I was just in the neighborhood and thought I'd stop by."

She'd heard that one before. "What are you really doing here?"

His smile dropped, and she immediately felt churlish for being so abrupt with him. "I'm sorry. Please come in."

The smile immediately returned, making her wonder if she had just committed herself to something she might regret. "I just have to finish up what I was doing. I hope you don't mind."

"Not at all."

He followed her into the kitchen and sat in one of the chairs while she picked up the electric mixer and finished off the whipping cream.

"What are you making?"

"I might have found an alternative for you instead of those chocolate dessert squares." She tried to keep the blush out of her cheeks but felt them heat up anyway. "I first wanted to do it myself to be sure it was something you could handle."

Carolyn held her breath, waiting for his reaction to her lack of confidence in his ability.

"That's very nice of you. I appreciate it." He folded his hands on the table and smiled.

Carolyn opened her mouth, but nothing came out.

When she got home from school earlier, the first thing she had done was to continue searching through more cookbooks for the elusive chocolate dessert square recipe she had tried to find a few days ago. Instead, she'd come across something similar that looked really good, and before she thought about what she was doing, she had started making the recipe.

He watched her in silence as she added the whipped cream to the cooled creme mixture. The uncharacteristic silence and his constant goofy smile unnerved her so much that she threw herself into teacher mode.

"You've already learned how to fold ingredients together versus stirring. You do the same thing here to mix the whipping cream in with the filling. It's kind of tricky because you have to make the filling by adding everything individually, at the right time, in a double boiler. Here." She dipped a spoon into the filling to give him a taste.

He closed his eyes as he savored the rich chocolate cream filling. "Mmmm. This is great."

Carolyn waited for him to say more, but he only sat there and smiled at her. "Mitchell, are you feeling okay?"

He continued with his insipid grin. "Just fine. Why do you ask?"

"No reason," she mumbled, then busied herself in spreading the filling on the first layer.

Mitchell continued to watch. It didn't take long before she couldn't stand the silence. "You said you were in the neighborhood. Where exactly were you?"

He smiled again as he spoke. "At the mall."

Any other day, Mitchell would not only have expounded on what he purchased, he would have also shown her and explained in full detail.

She placed the second layer on top of the filling, then began spreading again. "I read in the paper they're going to be renovating the mall, expanding and modernizing it and maybe even adding a second level."

"That's nice. What's a double boiler?"

"And I hear they're putting in a new. . ." Carolyn blinked at the abrupt change of subject and tried to figure how long it had been since she'd mentioned the double boiler. "A double boiler is for cooking or melting heat-sensitive items that are prone to scorching. It's kind of an inaccurate name, because the water shouldn't actually be boiling, as that's too hot." Rather than explain, she rested the spreader on the side of the bowl and picked up the double boiler from the stove, where she had left it, separating the top, which still held a few dribbles of the filling mixture, and held the set up for him to see. "This is a double boiler."

"That's just two pots."

"They stack. First you put water in the bottom one and then. . ." Carolyn let her voice trail off. He hadn't come for a cooking lesson tonight. However, she didn't know what he really had come for.

She put the pieces back together, returned them to the stovetop, picked up the spreader tool again, and started mindlessly spreading the remaining filling. "How's your mom doing? Is she getting ready for the big day?"

He shrugged his shoulders. "Ellen says Mom's getting crabby. She says the cast is awkward and itchy, but I know she's enjoying the attention."

Carolyn waited for him to expound on the wedding plans, but nothing came out. She placed the last layer on top and began to spread the last of the filling.

"Mitchell, are you sure nothing is wrong?"

"No, everything is right. Just right."

"Then why are you looking at me like that?"

"I'm trying to figure out where to take you for dinner tonight."

"Dinner?"

"Yes, dinner. I hope you haven't eaten yet. I haven't, and I was thinking about asking you to go somewhere soft and romantic. Somewhere we can talk. Unless you already have other plans."

Her eyes opened wide. She didn't want to go somewhere to talk to him—not when he was acting so strangely. And she certainly didn't want to go anywhere romantic, but she couldn't lie to him. She didn't have plans. "How about Pedro's? I haven't had Mexican food for a long time."

"Pedro's? But that's so loud and crowded."

"I know, but the food is great. I'm really craving enchiladas. And I hear they have a new mariachi band that's really good."

He blinked twice in rapid succession, then crossed his arms over his chest. "Are you serious?"

Carolyn nodded quickly. "I heard it's really good. And you don't need a reservation if you go early enough."

"That's not exactly what I had in mind."

Carolyn nodded so fast her glasses slid down the bridge of her nose. She pushed them up and kept talking without giving him time to protest. "We'll have to go now to get a good table. I think we're both dressed appropriately for Pedro's."

"Now wait a minute. I don't think—"

She rose and quickly set the bowl into the fridge, spoon and all. Without breaking her movement, she grabbed Mitchell's hand and started leading him to the door. "I can show you how to make that dessert another time. Suddenly I'm really hungry and really want to hear that new mariachi band. I just love the way they play those brass horns, don't you?"

"But—"

"Oops. Wait here. I have to get something."

Before he could reply, Carolyn ran into the bathroom and tossed the package of antacids into her purse, something she'd learned the hard way from her last visit to Pedro's.

Desperate times called for desperate measures.

❧

Mitchell stared glumly at himself in his bathroom mirror, covered his stomach with one hand, and burped, making no effort to hold it back. The release of pressure didn't give him the relief he needed, and the taste of jalapeño peppers still tainted his mouth. He dumped another couple of antacids into his palm and popped them into his mouth just as Jake appeared behind him in the bathroom doorway.

"Did I hear you correctly? What did you do last night?"

Mitchell shook his head to try to clear the ringing in his ears. "I said we went to Pedro's and got a table right next to the band."

"The Mitchell Farris I know hates brass bands and can't stand real spicy food. Are you my roommate's evil twin?"

He burped again. "Shut up, Jake."

Jake shrugged his shoulders, unaffected. "Just checking."

Mitchell grumbled something rather impolite, but Jake ignored him.

"You were with Carolyn, the cooking teacher, right? I have a feeling there's more cooking there than food."

Mitchell pulled out his shaver. "Don't you have somewhere to go?"

Jake let out a boisterous laugh and left, leaving Mitchell alone in the house.

Last night had been a night to remember, although not in the way he would have preferred. Besides the fact that everything was far too spicy and it wasn't the private, romantic evening he'd planned, they had thoroughly enjoyed themselves over dinner. The band wasn't what he normally enjoyed, but Carolyn had, and for now, that was what mattered.

Even though he hadn't had the opportunity to talk to Carolyn about where he wanted their relationship to go or give her the ring, some good did come out of the evening. Since she had chosen the table right next to the band, he had moved his chair to sit beside Carolyn so they could watch the band while they played. He'd snuggled in beside her and held her soft little hand while she listened to the music. For his part, he had been thinking of someplace more romantic he could take her another time.

His bubble had burst when he took her home and she disappeared inside without letting him kiss her good night. Still, the fact that she had held his hand encouraged him. And no matter how slowly things were progressing, they were progressing.

He dumped dog chow into Killer's bowl and sat at the table to eat his own breakfast while Killer happily crunched hers beside him. He poured himself a large glass of cold milk to settle his stomach.

After he brushed his teeth, only one thing remained to do before he left.

Mitchell sat on the couch and prayed. Once again, he asked for guidance and maturity in his relationship with Carolyn, and he prayed for assurance that it was God's will, not just his own, that they would be together. He didn't know exactly what Carolyn was seeking in the man whom she would one day fall in love with and marry, but he prayed that he could be everything she needed and wanted.

She was certainly everything he needed and wanted. She was kind and gentle, yet held her own in trying times. She had certainly been braver than he had been in the skirmish with the killer mouse. Carolyn also possessed charm and a quick wit, which he enjoyed immensely. He didn't know what kind of activities she pursued on a routine basis, but so far what they had done together had been mutually enjoyable.

Again, he prayed for God to show him the right path.

When he was done, he grabbed his jacket and left. Today, whatever he did with Carolyn, it would be somewhere quiet, without a crowd.

An hour later, he found himself at the gopher enclosure at the zoo, Carolyn at his side, unable to figure out what convoluted process had gotten him there. Absently, his hand rose to pat the little ring still in the pouch, safely nestled in his pocket.

"Oh, look! They want my popcorn!"

"Carolyn, the sign says not to feed them."

She sighed and Mitchell smiled. Not only was he getting used to her cute little sighs, he was becoming adept at predicting them.

She pointed to one of the big gophers, which was sitting up on its haunches, looking at them. "Look at his face. He's so cute. I wonder if they practice so people will feed them."

"I don't think gophers practice being cute. They're too stupid to practice anything."

He received a smack on the arm for his knowledgeable deduction.

After an unreasonable length of time watching the gophers balance on their fat, pampered bottoms, they continued on their way.

When Carolyn tossed her empty popcorn bag into the garbage can, she inhaled deeply and raised her hands. "Spring is in the air!" she exclaimed as she twirled around.

Mitchell pulled his jacket collar tighter. Wind was in the air, and it was nippy. "That's not spring. It's manure. We're next to the pony rides."

He received another smack on the arm for his comment.

They kept walking, pausing for a few minutes to look at each animal as they wandered through the zoo.

When they stopped in front of the bighorn sheep enclosure, a large number of the magnificent animals grazed and a few bleated their opinions of whatever it was sheep thought about.

As Carolyn stood to watch, Mitchell rested his hands on her shoulders, then shuffled right behind her so they were pressed together.

Carolyn tilted her neck to look up and back at him. "What are you doing?"

"I'm sheltering you from the wind so you'll stay warm."

She sighed again but didn't pull away, which he took as a positive sign.

A blast of wind came up from behind. Carolyn wrapped her arms around herself but otherwise didn't move. In an effort to warm himself, Mitchell dipped his head forward and nuzzled his face into the top of her head.

A pleasant herbal scent filled his nostrils. Mitchell closed his eyes and inhaled deeply in an effort to commit this moment to his memory forever.

Everything around them drifted into oblivion as he nuzzled Carolyn's forehead through her hair. The zoo in itself may not have been the most romantic place in the world, but where he was standing now, so close to her, touching her, it suddenly held a lot of promise he hadn't acknowledged before. The setting was casual, but he'd never been so close to her when she was relaxed, and all around them was quiet. She smiled up at him, and he was lost.

Very slowly, his fingers lifted from her shoulder to tip her chin up a wee bit higher. He leaned slightly forward, lowered his head, and kissed her lips. The position was a little awkward, but it was worth it to kiss her. The air around them was cool, but he ignored it for the heat of kissing Carolyn.

"Mommy, what are they doing?"

At the child's words, Carolyn pulled herself away and stepped forward to rest her hands on the railing, putting an inordinate amount of concentration on watching the sheep.

The mother's voice immediately followed the child's. "The boy sheep are butting heads. It's what sheep do to see who is the biggest and strongest of the herd."

"Why do they have to fight to do that?"

"Because the winner wants to be the husband of the prettiest lady sheep."

The little boy continued to ask countless questions about the sheep. Slowly, Mitchell approached Carolyn.

She glanced over her shoulder at the sound of his footsteps. "That shouldn't have happened, Mitchell."

"He wasn't looking at us. He was looking at the sheep." He reached out to touch her shoulder, but she shuffled away.

"It's not okay. This is a public place."

The only public around them was one small boy and his mother, who were now discussing what sheep ate for breakfast on school days; but if it bothered Carolyn, he wanted to respect her feelings. "You're right. I'm sorry. Would you like to keep going and see the rest of the animals?"

She nodded, so they continued their journey through the

zoo; but for the rest of the day, he didn't make any attempt to hold her hand or touch her in any way. Eventually the tension left her, and they were able to enjoy the zoo as they had before the sheep enclosure. One thing he knew. After they left, he would never be able to think of sheep without remembering their kiss.

On their way out, since they had to exit through the gift shop, Mitchell decided to buy her something so she would remember the entire day as fondly as he knew he would. While Carolyn browsed at the souvenir T-shirts, Mitchell made his selection.

He suspected he might have made the wrong choice when, while sitting in the car before they left the parking lot, he presented her with a stuffed plush sheep.

He bit his bottom lip as she held it in her hand, staring at the poor thing like it was made of something toxic.

"Come on, you've got to admit it's cute."

"It's cute," she mumbled.

"And it's nice and soft."

Cautiously, she petted it, then smiled just enough to give Mitchell some faint glimmer of hope. "Yes, it's soft."

"It's cuddly, too. Just like me."

She whacked him over the head with it before he had a chance to raise his arms.

On the way home, they chatted about the animals they had seen—every animal except the sheep.

His plan to give her the ring today didn't quite work out, but he'd managed to give her something else as a reminder of their time together. With any luck, tomorrow would present a better opportunity.

Again, she didn't give him a chance to kiss her at the door, but before the door closed, he did have the chance to say that he would pick her up for church, and she didn't turn him down.

Mitchell smiled the entire way home. As always, God had provided a way.

nine

"Good evening, everyone. We've got a lot of things to do today, so let's get started quickly."

Carolyn prepared the pastry dough, warning everyone to work slowly to prevent it from tearing during the rolling process. She specifically cautioned Mitchell that too much handling would make it tough, but he took being singled out with a smile and a wink.

Next, she demonstrated making the strudel, rolling it and shaping it, and showing how it was different than the previous project, then sent everyone to their kitchenettes to do it themselves.

As she walked from group to group, several times conversations stopped. Carolyn had already noticed many of the ladies glancing back and forth between herself and Mitchell all evening, and the combination gave her cause for concern. It appeared many of her class members thought she and Mitchell were an item.

Even though she hadn't meant it that way, Carolyn now realized that she had fueled their thoughts when she kissed him on the cheek in front of the class. She'd only meant it in jest, but it had backfired on her. And, if the class took it the wrong way, she was afraid to think of how Mitchell felt.

She certainly didn't want to encourage him in whatever it was he thought he was doing by hanging around her so much. It was neither fair nor realistic for her to be spending so much time with him. She hoped and prayed that her actions had not given him the wrong impression, but she feared they had.

The truth was, she really didn't know exactly how she felt about Mitchell. She would have been lying if she tried to tell herself she didn't like him; but she was more than ready for a permanent relationship. Such a relationship had to be based on more than simply liking someone and being easily amused by them.

She forced herself to ignore the whisperings and pushed the class forward. Soon, everything was done, and the only person left to clean up his mess was Mitchell. He tucked the last baking sheet away as Carolyn gathered up her purse, bag of utensils, and cookbook and headed for the door.

The cupboard door closed with a bang, and his footsteps echoed behind her. "Can I walk you out?"

"The custodian will be watching to make sure I get to my car safely," she called over her shoulder, not slowing her pace.

"But I need to talk to you."

She didn't want to talk to him. She was too afraid she would weaken if he started talking about anything besides cooking, which he probably would, since cooking class was over.

"I'm sorry, but I have to go," she mumbled, not slowing her pace.

Carolyn didn't slow down until she reached the friendly custodian, who was standing dutifully beside the door. She nodded and mumbled a good night to Mr. O'Sullivan as he held the door open and she stepped outside into the brisk night air. Out of the corner of her eye, she saw Mitchell starting to exit, as well.

"Hold on, young man, wait a minute."

Mr. O'Sullivan blocked the path to the exit. Mitchell's sneakers squeaked on the tile floor as he stopped abruptly. Carolyn kept walking.

"I think I recognize you. Didn't you used to attend here?"

"Uh, yeah, I did, but—"

"Wait. Farris, right? I ran into those friends of yours at the coffee shop, Gordie Reid and Roland Carruthers. I remember the time the three of you—"

"Carolyn! Wait!"

She ignored his plea and quickened her step, managing to reach her car before Mitchell disengaged himself. She threw everything in without regard to neatness and drove off.

As soon as she arrived home, she dropped her bag on the kitchen counter, but instead of putting everything in its rightful place, she began to pace.

Things were getting out of hand, and she didn't know what to do about it.

She didn't know how it happened, but she'd been seeing Mitchell almost every day, starting not long after they met. It wasn't supposed to be this way, yet when she hadn't seen him Monday, she'd missed him.

It didn't make sense.

She was at a point in her life where she had to move forward with her future. She was settled into her career as a teacher. She was well involved in her church and the various activities there, and she was satisfied in her walk with the Lord. All else considered, only one very important thing was lacking in her life. From the bottom of her heart, she desired a special man who would love her the same way she loved him. And following that, she wanted to start a family.

She wanted to trust that God knew what was best for her and that whoever He sent would be the man she could be happy with for the rest of her time on earth. She'd even started praying for God to send such a man not long ago, and it was about that time God had sent Hank into her life. Yet as much as Hank matched all the things she was looking for in a husband, Hank had made it known he wasn't ready for marriage.

She thought the answer was simply to get to know Hank better, and the relationship God planned for them to have would work itself out over time. Yet, instead of spending her time with Hank and developing things there, she found herself spending nearly all her free time with Mitchell, a man who was wrong for her in every way that she could see.

Carolyn closed her eyes to pray for direction when the sudden jangle of the phone startled her. With a trembling hand, she picked up the receiver.

"I think we should talk. You ran off on me."

"Mitchell," she stammered. "We both have work in the morning. It's late."

"It's not that late. I think you were avoiding me."

Carolyn squeezed her eyes shut, not wanting to tell him the truth but knowing she had to. "I think the class is starting to make assumptions about us. . . ." She let her voice trail off.

She waited for him to say something, but he was strangely silent for the longest time. When he finally spoke, his voice was strangely soft. "Tomorrow is Bible study night. You promised me that this week we could go together again."

Her heart pounded in her chest. If it hadn't been for that promise, she would have told him she'd changed her mind. Hank had promised her that he would be a regular attendee at the meetings, but in the last few months, he'd only been to one. She knew what it felt like to have a promise broken, and she couldn't do that to Mitchell.

"All right. Pick me up at seven."

"Great. Since we won't be cooking, let's go out for dinner, too. Oops. Killer's outside barking. You're right; it is getting late. I can't let her disturb the neighborhood. Gotta run. Bye."

The dial tone sounded in her ear before she completely mumbled her good-bye.

She lowered the phone to its cradle and buried her face in her hands. What had she done?

ten

Mitchell rang Carolyn's doorbell and raised his hand to wiggle his tie, then patted the pocket containing the little ring.

God's timing was perfect. After Tuesday's class, he had started to get a little nervous; but even though they rushed to be on time for the Bible study on Wednesday, they'd had a lovely dinner.

Mitchell smiled to himself. Tonight, neither of them had anything else to do, and neither had to get up early in the morning. Later, over candlelight and a juicy steak dinner, he would give her the little ring and tell her that he was falling in love.

The door opened. "Hi, Mitchell. Come in."

He wiggled the unaccustomed knot at his neck. "Sorry I'm so late. I often get stuck working overtime on Fridays."

"I'm finding that out, aren't I?" She smiled, and his heart rate kicked up a notch. Instead of her favorite fuzzy pink sweater and denim skirt, tonight she wore a pretty light purple dress and matching colored shoes that made her a little taller than usual.

His smile widened. "You look nice."

Her cheeks darkened, which he thought was kind of cute. It also told him she didn't hear enough compliments, something that was about to change. "Thank you. I was wondering, after dinner, would you like to see a movie? I saw a commercial for a new comedy that looked really good."

Taking a woman to a movie after dinner sounded more like a real date than ever, but he wasn't going to point that out quite yet.

He checked his watch. "I'd like that, but I think it's a little late to do both. What time is the late showing?"

"I don't know. Maybe we should check the paper."

Instead of taking Carolyn out to the car, he sauntered into the living room and planted himself on her couch while she spread the newspaper on the coffee table.

"Here it is. It starts at. . ." Her voice trailed off, and she pressed her finger to the newspaper. "Mitchell! Look!"

The sudden voice inflection made him jump. He leaned forward and looked at where her finger was planted.

"It's the Annual Cooking and Kitchen Showcase! It's this weekend, and the doors open at nine tomorrow morning!" As they made eye contact, the sparkle in her eyes disappeared. Her voice dropped. "Never mind." She turned back to the paper.

"What do you mean, never mind?"

"It's too late to ask anyone to go with me. I guess there's always next year."

Mitchell grinned. After all he'd learned about cooking in the past month, Mitchell thought that perhaps there might be something to interest him, too. "I'll go with you. It's probably just like the marketplace, and that was fun."

Her lips tightened. "It's not really like that at all, Mitchell."

"Even better. Something different will be fun."

Her head tipped to one side, and one eye narrowed. "Are you sure?"

"Sure. Why not?"

"Tickets are cheaper if you buy them in advance."

"Okay."

Before he could think about it, she rested her finger on the phone number listed in the ad, mumbled it a few times to memorize it, and ran into the kitchen. By the time he realized that she was paying for the tickets over the phone with her credit card, it was too late to do anything about it.

He stood when he heard her hang up. "I must be more tired than I thought. I didn't realize what you were going to do. I wanted to pay for those."

"Nonsense. It was my idea, so I'm paying. But if you want to appease your bruised ego, you can pay for my dinner tonight."

"I was going to pay for your dinner anyway. Where do you want to go?"

"Pedro's."

"No." He shook his head so fast that a lock of hair fell onto his forehead. "Anywhere but there." He rested his hand on his stomach. He'd felt the effects of that one dinner for two days afterward. He'd taken every last one of Jake's antacids before he felt normal.

"Please? It's the last night before the mariachi band moves on to another city."

He opened his mouth to protest, but her pleading eyes stopped him. "I give up. But before we go, I have to stop at the drug store for something."

ಜ

"Look at all the cars," Mitchell grumbled as he turned into a parking spot that had to be at least two miles from the main entrance. He estimated about a thousand cars in the parking lot, and the line of people waiting for the doors to open was already around the corner of the building.

By the time they waited in line and picked up their reserved tickets at the entrance, another five hundred people had lined up behind them. They were each given programs listing all the display booths, a list of seminars, and a map. The enticing aroma of fresh coffee wafted through the air, teasing him. He'd been careful with his selections at Pedro's last night, and he'd had an extra dose of antacids before he left, so now he was more than ready for a large cup of hot coffee.

They stood to the side to look at the map and figure out the layout of the building. He'd almost figured out where the coffee concession was when Carolyn's hand blocked his view, pointing to a list at the side of the printed form. "We get one free class with the purchase of an advance ticket, so I signed up for this one." Her finger rested on some French person's name he couldn't attempt to pronounce. She looked up at him, blushed, then pointed to another seminar, a demonstration on some food item he couldn't pronounce either, even if he did know what it was, which he didn't. "I didn't know what you'd be interested in, but I signed you up for this one. If you don't want to go, I'll go instead."

He smiled. "It's all yours. Enjoy yourself."

She turned and pointed to an area in the far corner of the building. "There's a big screen television there for the guys. You can go there while I'm in the sessions, if you want. They last forty-five minutes each."

Mitchell grinned. A guy area. Perfect. He hoped they had a large coffeepot. "Let's start walking and see how much we can take in before your first class. How long until it starts?"

"We only have an hour, so we'd better get going."

"Only?" Mitchell scanned the area, trying to figure out what was here that would take more than an hour to see. In a room full of mainly women, he stood a head taller than most of the people there, so he could easily see almost everything. According to the map, there were hundreds of booths and displays, in addition to demonstration areas and rooms for the class sessions. He'd never seen anything like it. The annual auto show was nothing like this. However, since he couldn't imagine there could be that many ways to cook a meal, he figured that, unlike the auto show, they would be out of the cooking convention within a couple of hours, including her lectures.

Before they moved, he reached for her hand.

When she looked up at him, he gave it a gentle squeeze to stop her from protesting. "We don't want to get separated."

"Okay. Let's go this way first."

The first section was called Microwave Cooking. They managed to walk past the first booth with a cursory glance, but Carolyn stopped at the second one. They watched two women showing some kind of gadget that cooked rice in a microwave, then had to wait while everyone tasted a small white paper cup full of the fresh cooked rice, followed by sufficient oohing and aahing about how tender it was. Then everyone, including Carolyn, walked away without buying one. Carolyn led him by the hand to the next booth, which was also preparing some kind of food and handing out samples. He was going to suggest that if she was hungry, they could go to the food court to buy something that was more than one nibble at a time, but Carolyn's attention was glued to the demonstration.

By the end of the hour, Mitchell had learned more about how to cook things in the microwave with strange utensils than he wanted to know in a lifetime. Worst of all, he was still hungry even though he'd eaten so many samples he'd lost count.

As he stood waiting while Carolyn inspected the latest and greatest version of some gadget he couldn't identify, Mitchell glanced around him. There weren't many men present, but those he had seen with their wives or girlfriends looked as bored as he felt.

"It's almost time for my first course. Shall we meet back here at ten forty-five?"

Mitchell looked up as a man pushing a stroller with an infant in it walked in the direction of the guy area.

He synchronized his watch with Carolyn's. "Gotcha. Ten forty-five."

⁊

Carolyn hurried off toward the meeting room area. She could tell Mitchell was as bored as she predicted he would be, but he was being a good sport about it. However, just because she had warned him in advance didn't make her feel any better. Because of the guilt, she'd separated from him at the last possible second, which meant the only seats left were in the back.

She pulled her notepad out of her purse and adjusted her glasses as the class began. The chef displayed culinary techniques she could only dream of, making her wish she had more flair in the kitchen or, failing that, a specialty she could be proud of. The demonstration ended before she realized the time had gone by, and she enthusiastically joined the rest of the audience in a healthy round of applause. On her way out, she picked up a bag containing the recipe the chef had prepared—as if she could ever prepare it with such skill—a small booklet promoting the chef's newly released cookbook, and a small taste sample of today's demonstration.

Mitchell was already waiting for her by the time she reached the appointed meeting place. He held a steaming cup of coffee in one hand and a large bag in the other.

"Was there something interesting on television?"

He grinned then shook his head. "I didn't make it that far. Look what I bought."

Carolyn took one look at the bag and read the logo. "Oh, no," she groaned under her breath. "You didn't."

"It's a Handy Dandy Veggie-O-Matic Chopper. You should see what it does."

Carolyn forced herself to smile. She should never have left him alone. She should have personally escorted him to the men's area in the back and told him to stay put.

"It slices and dices and chops and everything. It even makes French fries, and you should have tasted them. Were they ever good."

She highly doubted Mitchell would ever attempt to make French fries from scratch, and it would be a pretty good guess that he didn't own a deep fryer. "Mitchell, when are you ever going to use such an item?"

He shrugged his shoulders. "I don't know. But when I do, I'll do the job in record time."

"I think that in a few years the Salvation Army will have a wonderful donation, still in the original packaging."

He ignored her as he dropped the chopper back into the bag and picked up a long, narrow box. "And look at this. I saw the guy cut a PVC pipe with this knife, and you should have seen how cleanly it cut through a big fat tomato after that. You said I needed a good knife."

Carolyn shook her head in disbelief. "Have you ever been to anything like this before?"

He dug through the bag as he spoke. "I go to the auto show every year, if that's what you mean."

"No, I mean something like this, where there are things to actively participate in, demos, door prizes, and booths with a million things for sale."

He stuck his head down closer to the bag opening, continuing to rifle through the contents until he found the specific item he was searching for. "No, never," he mumbled.

Carolyn didn't know whether to laugh or cry as she watched Mitchell pull out an assortment of gadgets, some of which might be handy to her but would be totally useless to Mitchell once he had finished the cooking class.

When he finished, she sighed and shook her head. "Come on. We still have a lot to see."

She grabbed his hand and led him to a section where his wallet would be safe. Together they nibbled samples and wandered around until they ended up at the food court. Carolyn couldn't stuff in another bite after everything she'd eaten, but Mitchell bought himself a corn dog on a stick, and they kept walking.

A scratchy voice she could barely understand boomed over the loudspeaker announcing the other session she'd signed up for was starting in five minutes. She tried to calculate how long it would take to escort Mitchell safely to the men's area and still be on time but knew she would never make it.

Guiding him to the side so people could walk around them, she held tightly to both his hands, forcing him to make eye contact. "Please, Mitchell, promise me you won't buy anything while I'm gone, okay?"

He held up one hand. "Promise. Scout's honor," he said while making the appropriate hand signal.

She didn't know if he had ever been a Boy Scout but didn't have the time to challenge him on it. "I'll meet you back here when it's over, okay?"

"Sure."

She dropped his hands and dashed off. Again, she had to

sit in the back, but it had been worth it to extract a promise out of Mitchell.

The demonstration on Pâté Feuilletee was fascinating, but while she picked up some wonderful tips, Mitchell was always in the back of her mind. She left the room as soon as she could, missing the opportunity to ask the chef a few questions, and hurried to the appointed meeting place where, once again, Mitchell was waiting.

"What did you do this time while I was gone?" She was almost afraid to ask, but she had to know.

"Nothing bad. I didn't buy anything. I just entered my name in a bunch of free draws."

"Oh, no. Mitchell, they're going to phone and tell you that you won something, except you have to buy something or watch a demonstration for two hours to claim your prize, which is never worth the cost of getting there. And then they sell the names they've collected to mailing lists."

He shrugged his shoulders. "I don't care. I'd never buy anything I didn't really need."

Carolyn almost choked but held back her comment. "Come on. Over there, they're featuring a selection of new products for people with food allergies."

He checked his watch. "We've been here over seven hours. You mean there's still something we haven't seen?"

"Just two sections. If you want to go sit down and watch television, I don't mind."

"No. If I wanted to watch television, I would have stayed home. I came here to be with you."

Carolyn's throat tightened. By now, most of the men who had accompanied their wives and girlfriends were in the men's area, many of them having consumed far too much beer. Yet except for the time she'd spent in class, Mitchell hadn't left her side. Many times, when he didn't think she was looking, she'd glanced up to see him staring blankly at nothing, obviously bored to death, but he never complained.

"Forget the other two sections. I think we've seen enough,

and I'm tired anyway. Let's go home."

His relief was almost tangible, and Carolyn knew she'd done the right thing.

On the way out, they passed a booth selling the same vegetable chopper he had purchased earlier in the day. He grinned and pointed but didn't slow down. "I got mine cheaper."

"It's only a bargain if you actually use it."

He laughed and held the door open as they left the building and began the long walk back to the car.

"I'm hungry. Can we go somewhere for supper?"

Carolyn rested one hand on her stomach. She'd consumed so many samples, she didn't think she'd be able to eat for a week. "I couldn't eat another bite, but if you're hungry, let's go through the drive-through."

"The drive-through? But. . ." Mitchell's hand drifted to the breast pocket of his leather jacket, he patted something tucked inside, then rammed his hands in his pockets as they walked. "I guess so," he mumbled.

They trudged in silence the rest of the way to the car, but once they were on the road going home, Carolyn could no longer contain herself. "Did you see that lady who was making the crepes? And how thin she could make them with that fancy pan?"

Mitchell checked for traffic over his shoulder. "Uh, yeah."

"And those tiny sausage rolls made on that specialty rack that fit into a toaster oven? I couldn't care less about the rack, but I wonder where those sausages came from. They were absolutely delicious and not dripping with fat."

"They were okay."

"And those brownies made in that special pan in the microwave. I've never been able to make cake with a decent texture in the microwave. But you know what was the most ridiculous thing I saw? That potato peeler tub thing, where you run water into it and between the water itself and the water pressure turning the grating unit inside, it peels the potatoes by itself. I timed it. Could you imagine taking fifteen minutes to peel potatoes?"

"I guess not."

When Carolyn didn't speak, silence hung in the air. Other than the soft music droning from the CD player and the hum of the traffic, the car was quiet.

"Mitchell, are you okay?"

"Huh? What? Oh, I'm fine. I'm just tremendously underwhelmed with the wonders of the modern kitchen. I didn't know what I was missing."

Not sure if his sarcasm was meant as a joke or not, Carolyn said nothing. After a few minutes of silence, she made a few more comments about things she'd seen, but he continued to respond with few words. When silence hung in the air periodically, he kept reaching to his breast pocket, feeling something, and then dropping his hand back to the steering wheel, making Carolyn wonder if he'd recently quit smoking.

Closer to home, he pulled into the drive-through of the local hamburger joint and ordered. Carolyn held the warm bag in her lap until they pulled into her driveway.

Carolyn made a pot of herbal tea while Mitchell ate the burger and fries, and then they moved into the living room.

Mitchell sat in the middle of the couch, which meant Carolyn had to sit beside him.

Carolyn stretched and wiggled her toes before sagging fully into the soft cushions. "I didn't realize my feet were so sore or that I was so tired until now."

Mitchell shifted his weight so she sank in his direction. "Same."

She flipped the television on for lack of something better to do. "I can't believe the time. We spent the whole day there."

"I can believe it."

She turned toward him. "Thank you for taking me, especially on short notice. I really had a wonderful time."

He smiled and slipped his arm around her back, drawing her against him. "It's also nice to be able to sit and relax with a good friend after it's all over, too."

Carolyn smiled back. She didn't think it appropriate for "a

good friend" to have his arm around her, but she was so tired, she couldn't help snuggling into his warmth.

She thought of his words. If she had to put a label to what was happening between them, then calling Mitchell a friend was safe and probably quite accurate. She'd never before come to know someone so quickly or so easily. She already knew most of Mitchell's likes and dislikes, the movies he liked to watch, and the books he liked to read. She'd learned a lot about his job and told him a lot about hers. She enjoyed his quirky sense of humor, and she'd even started to miss him when they weren't together.

"Yes, this is nice," she muttered and sighed as she let herself continue to relax. "I'm so tired. I think it's tripled in size since last year."

He mumbled a reply she couldn't understand, and Carolyn didn't ask him to repeat it. Instead, she let herself relax even more with the steady and soothing rhythm of his breathing. Her eyes drifted shut of their own accord. She would open them in a minute.

She shifted with the movement as he reached up and patted his shirt pocket. Mitchell's voice sounded deeper when she was pressed up against him. "I was wondering. I've really enjoyed going with you to your Bible studies and church on Sunday morning. I'd like it if we went together all the time. What do you think?"

"Mmm."

"Was that a yes or a no? Carolyn?"

She wanted to answer, but she couldn't. All she felt was peace as everything faded into softness and warmth.

eleven

Beeping sounded, jolting Carolyn from a sound sleep. She opened her eyes and started to roll over, squinting to focus on the time.

The clock was missing. And she wasn't in bed. She was on the living room couch.

As soon as she gained her bearings, she located the source of the beeping, which was a man's watch, lying on the coffee table. She picked up her glasses, which were beside the watch, and put them on.

Eight thirty.

Carolyn blinked, trying to figure everything out, starting with what day it was. The last thing she remembered was watching television with Mitchell after attending the Kitchen Showcase.

Her stomach churned. She'd fallen asleep on the couch. She clutched her blanket, which was the one from her bed, and glanced to her side. He'd also brought her pillow.

The warmth in her cheeks escalated to a burn when she found a note, next to where the watch had been.

Good morning, Sleepyhead!
I hope you had a good night's sleep. I had to use your keys to lock up when I left, so I'll be back for church in the morning. Expect me at 9:15. I'll bring breakfast.

Love, Mitchell

Carolyn buried her face in her hands. The thought of Mitchell tucking her in at night, even if it was just on the couch, made her cringe with embarrassment.

Without wasting any more time, Carolyn bolted off the

couch, heading straight for the bathroom. She didn't know how she was going to get ready before Mitchell arrived.

She'd barely finished applying her mascara when the door-bell rang.

Mitchell stood in the doorway holding a brown paper bag in one hand and a cardboard holder containing two steaming cups in the other. He smiled brightly. "Good morning. Sleep well? You look nice. That color really suits you."

Carolyn opened her mouth, but no words came out.

"Aren't you going to let me in? I have food. And coffee."

She shuffled to the side to give him room to pass. "Of course."

Mitchell walked straight past her into the kitchen, but her feet remained glued to the floor. She didn't want to share breakfast in the kitchen with Mitchell. She didn't know how she was going to sit across the table from him and carry on an intelligent conversation.

When he was halfway through the living room, he stopped and turned around to smile so sweetly that she nearly cried. "Don't worry, you didn't snore or do anything embarrassing. Come on, before everything gets cold. These fast-food hot-cakes are bad enough when they're warm."

Cold food was the least of her worries. Somehow she managed to talk to him while they ate their breakfast, although by the time she got to the last mouthful, it tasted like cardboard.

Sharing breakfast with him was one more reminder of how much Mitchell had become ingrained in her life.

Her friends now expected him regularly at the Wednesday night Bible study, and they asked about him when he wasn't with her on Sunday, whether Hank was there or not—which was rare. Her night school class definitely thought of them as a couple. Even his dog liked her.

Now they would be attending Sunday service together, again.

Mitchell rose and went into the living room to pick up his watch. "I guess it's time to go," he said as he walked back into the kitchen. "Are we going to your church or mine? I don't think I've been to my own church for over a month."

Carolyn sighed. She was too tired to meet new people, even though it meant that the entire congregation would be seeing her with Mitchell on yet another Sunday. "It's getting late. We can go to your church next weekend."

Carolyn bit her lip, but it was too late. The words had already been said.

"That's a good idea. You can also see it before the wedding. You are coming with me to Jake and Ellen's wedding, aren't you?"

"Uh. . ."

She opened her mouth to decline, but his eyes stopped her. She'd seen that look before, the day he begged her to give him remedial help with his cooking skills. She didn't want to go through that again.

Carolyn sighed again. "Sure."

"Before I forget, I can't see you for dinner tonight. I've got a family thing I have to do. Can we do dinner tomorrow night after work?"

Carolyn stood. There was no point in trying to decline. He would only bamboozle her into going out with him another time and another time after that.

When she sighed again, the corners of his mouth quivered.

"Yes, I'd like that."

Strangely, she meant it.

ॐ

Mitchell drummed his fingers on the steering wheel as he waited for the red light. If all the lights from here on out were green, then he had a chance of running into the cooking class on time—barely.

In the past, he had never minded the overtime. It wasn't like he ever had anything better to do, and the extra money on payday was always a treat. Now, he had changed his mind.

His supposed date last night with Carolyn hadn't happened. Just as he was about to leave, the dock foreman had come running in to say that someone had driven through the fence between their compound and the adjoining business. Not only did he have to call the police, but he also had to arrange to have someone come in at an unbelievable fee to fix the security fence at night. Then he had to deal with the police report and file charges, since there would be an insurance claim and criminal charges against the man who did the damages. Worst of all, he had to stay until the repair crew actually arrived and started working.

Instead of sharing an intimate dinner, he'd ordered a pizza, Carolyn heated up some leftovers, and they'd sat and talked on the phone while they ate, him at work and her at home. Again, he'd been unable to give her the ring, which seemed to have become a permanent fixture in his pocket.

He ran into the classroom to see Carolyn holding up some kind of gadget he'd seen at the cooking show, but he couldn't remember what it was called or what it was for.

The room suddenly went deathly quiet as he made his way to the only empty seat, which was in the exact center of the classroom—the same chair he'd sat in during the first class.

Without making a major production out of his late arrival, Carolyn held up a tray of food for all to see. "There was a question on the registration form asking if anyone here was allergic to seafood. Before we continue, does anyone here have allergies who may not have noticed the question on the form?"

When no one spoke up, Carolyn continued. "That's good. We're going to make battered shrimp, which will be dipped in various sauces. This works with many types of seafood, but shrimp is the most popular. It's much better to use fresh shrimp, so that's what we're going to do."

She then went through a gruesome process of pulling a shrimp apart, coating it with some stuff she mixed up, then frying it until it was cooked.

It smelled much better than it looked, and the mouth-watering aroma made Mitchell's stomach grumble—a nasty reminder that he hadn't had time to eat supper in his rush to get out of work and to class on time.

Carolyn then put together something else with a fancy name he couldn't pronounce and sent everyone to their kitchen units. As they got organized, she made the rounds to each kitchen, gave each person four shrimp, then returned to the demonstration table.

"Okay, everyone. As a change of pace, we're going to all do this together. Watch me, and we'll do it step by step."

Mitchell picked up one shrimp by the tail and examined it. He'd never seen a whole shrimp before. It wasn't what he'd expected. He thought shrimp were brown, but it was a grayish color.

"Is everyone ready?"

Several of the ladies around him nodded unenthusiastically.

"First you break off the legs, like this."

He did like she said, repeating in his mind that the poor creature was already dead and didn't feel a thing.

"Good. Now put your thumb and pointer finger at the point where the head meets the body and pull off the head."

If he was hungry before, he certainly wasn't now. His stomach contracted as he placed his fingers in the position Carolyn demonstrated.

"That's the worst part." Carolyn grinned, and he hoped she couldn't tell he felt sick. "The shell will peel right off quite easily now; just pull here and voilà!"

Mitchell pulled, but it didn't come out quite as easily as Carolyn's did. He pulled again and nearly dropped it at the unpleasant slimy feel of the thing inside. Canned shrimp didn't feel like this. He let it fall to the plate.

Carolyn held up her shrimp. "This next step is called deveining. Does everyone see that line down the back? Take your knife, make a quick slice down the back, and sort of scrape it out, like this."

Mitchell's stomach rolled. He sucked in a deep breath to stop it, but the smell of the raw seafood permeating the room only made it worse.

"You might think this is the shrimp's spinal cord, but it's

not. It's just an intestine."

"Just" an intestine. Mitchell worked to control his breathing.

"You don't have to remove it, but it makes a more pleasant-looking appetizer."

With shaking hands, Mitchell inserted the tip of the knife and slowly ran it along the line, but the slice didn't go as neatly as Carolyn's. Instead, it made a jagged tear, and the shrimp started to come apart in his hands. For a moment he considered running to his car, first to get a breath of fresh air and then to bring back his needle-nose pliers to hold the shrimp steady so he could get the job done faster.

Finally, he managed to lift the dark, threadlike vein out, but in pieces, not like Carolyn had done. As soon as he did, he laid the shrimp down and looked away. Carolyn was trying to get an overview of everyone's progress from the central location of the demonstration table, so he concentrated on her until his stomach settled.

"You all look like you're doing fine. Now do the other three. And when you're done, we'll heat up the frying pans, dip the shrimp in the batter, cook them for four minutes, and then you can all do the next project without me."

He struggled through disemboweling the other three shrimp, but with each one, the process became slightly less revolting. By the time he began to cook them, the aroma made his appetite return, and he could hardly wait to eat them.

As they reached the point halfway through the second project, his stomach was grumbling so loudly that Lorraine and Sarah were giggling, and Mrs. Finkleman felt so sorry for him that she snuck him one of her shrimp to eat before Carolyn gave them permission.

When that permission came, not only was he the first one finished eating, but he'd managed to mooch an extra shrimp from Lorraine and Sarah, as well.

As usual, he loitered when class was over until he was the last person out.

"I'm sorry I was late, Carolyn."

She hesitated for only a second, then continued packing up her area. "It's okay, Mitchell. I understand if you had to work late."

"Yeah, I did. I also haven't had supper, and I was wondering if you'd like to go grab a burger or something. The things we made today were good but not enough to constitute a real meal."

"I really can't, Mitchell. Believe it or not, I have a bunch of reports and tests to mark. Even the home ec department has to do them. I wish I could, but not today. How about tomorrow?"

His heart soared to think that she had suggested an alternate day, but just as quickly, his heart sank. "I can't. Our major competitor served strike notice today. That's why I had to work so late. Businesses can't afford to have their stuff tied up in a labor dispute, so a lot of people shifted over to us, and we weren't prepared. It will take a few more days before we've adjusted, and by then I'm sure the dispute will be settled and it will be back to normal. The way it looks, it's going to be like this all week."

"Then I guess I won't see you until the weekend."

"Yeah. It looks that way."

Mitchell raised his hand to his pocket. It was going to be a long week.

⁂

Carolyn shut off the vacuum cleaner and ran to the door. She didn't have to wait a second time to confirm that she was hearing correctly. In a way, she was almost expecting Mitchell. She didn't want to admit it, even to herself, but she hadn't seen him since the last cooking class, and she'd missed him.

She turned the lock and flung the door open. "Mi—Hank? What are you doing here?"

Hank stood before her with his raincoat open. Beneath it he wore his usual dark suit and matching tie, which she thought odd for a Saturday afternoon. In his hand was a bouquet of red roses.

"May I come in?"

She stood aside and ran her fingers through her hair to

straighten it and smoothed the folds out of her sweatshirt. "Certainly."

Hank walked past her with the flowers, then waited for her to close the door behind him, which she thought rather strange. If it were Mitchell, he would have given her the flowers, tried to kiss her, and he would have closed the door behind himself. She envisioned Mitchell's impish smile, but as she blinked, Hank's solemn face came into focus.

He cleared his throat. "I brought these for you." He held out the roses.

Hesitantly, she accepted the bouquet. The only time Hank had given her flowers had been a corsage at last year's Christmas banquet because she had sung a solo. Other than that, the only time he had given her anything was at Christmas and on her birthday. Her feet didn't move as she stared down at the flowers, wondering what the occasion was to warrant them.

He straightened his tie. "I've been giving this a lot of thought lately, and I'm asking if you'll marry me. I didn't buy you a ring because I thought you might want to pick one out for yourself."

The roses trembled as her hands started shaking. Perhaps she had strange expectations, but she had always thought a proposal was accompanied by words of love and affection, followed by a hug or a tender touch, even a kiss. It should have been a moment to be remembered fondly for the rest of a person's life. The suit and the flowers seemed so prepared, even calculated, and not very romantic, despite the proposal.

"I can see I've caught you off guard, and I can't blame you. Would you like to think about it for a few days?"

She nearly choked. Obviously, another grand misconception of hers was that the day a man asked her to marry him, she would have been overjoyed, filled with excitement and visions of a happy future together. She should want to scream a big yes and throw herself into his arms.

She didn't know what to say, but one thing she did know. She couldn't marry Hank. Not when she was in love with Mitchell.

As the thought hit home, Carolyn felt the color drain from her face.

"Carolyn, are you okay? You don't look well."

He was right. She didn't feel very well at all. She was in love but with the wrong man.

But even if she wasn't in love with Mitchell, she couldn't marry Hank. She'd always thought marriage was a fulfillment of love and commitment. If Hank truly loved her, she should have been able to tell by now. She suspected that if men had a biological clock, Hank's was ticking. His proposal had nothing to do with love. She wanted to get married, too, but she wasn't desperate enough to be trapped in a loveless marriage. She would rather live alone.

Carolyn cleared her throat to get her voice to work properly. "I'm sorry, Hank, but I can't marry you. I don't need time to think about it. I like you very much as a friend, but I don't think it would work."

He shoved his hands into his pockets. "Well. I see. To tell the truth, even though we haven't exactly had a hearts and flowers relationship, I thought we were compatible enough to get married and raise a family. After all, neither of us is getting any younger."

Carolyn felt sick. Compatible. She wondered if she was supposed to be flattered. The roses, which she had always thought were the flowers of love, felt like a sham in her hands. She didn't love him, nor did he love her. But yet, Hank possessed everything she'd ever wanted in a man. He was mature, carried himself with class and dignity, was a marvelous host, and had a wonderful career as an accountant for a large corporation. He chose his leisure activities with great care—golf for fitness and the theater or gallery for something educational. Often his choices had involved business contacts, which allowed her to meet his peers in a social environment.

Hank's biggest shortcoming was his attendance at church and Bible study meetings. And come to think of it, in all they discussed, they never seemed to talk about God's Word, not even the Sunday sermon topics. She didn't even know his favorite Bible verse. She didn't know if he had a favorite verse. The more she thought about it, while she knew he was a believer, she didn't know exactly how important God was in Hank's life.

She couldn't love a man who didn't love God first.

She was in love with Mitchell Farris. How could her Mr. Right be so very Mr. Wrong?

"I think you'd better leave. And take these with you." She stood and held out the flowers, but he didn't accept them.

Hank's face hardened, and his lips tightened into a scowl. "Go ahead and turn me down now, but before long you'll be begging my forgiveness. If you're lucky, I'll consider you again. Just wait. When you're closer to forty, you'll see that life is passing you by. By then it will be too late. I'll be married to someone else."

Her mouth dropped open then snapped shut. "Get out," she ground out between her teeth. She thrust the flowers back into his hand, but he dropped them to the floor and stomped out, slamming the door behind him. As she stood transfixed in one spot, his car started then roared off into the distance.

Carolyn continued to stare at the closed door long after the sound of Hank's car had disappeared, stunned that he had asked for her hand in marriage not on the basis of love, but because he considered them—at least her—almost past their prime marriage years. She wasn't twenty-four years old anymore, but neither was she too old to desire a marriage based on mutual love and children conceived and raised in that love.

Rather than being sorry that she would never see Hank again, she was glad he was gone.

Her gaze drifted to the roses lying in a jumbled pile in the middle of the hardwood floor. Many of the velvety petals had fallen off and a broken leaf lay to the side, the heady rose scent made stronger by their disarray. Slowly, she counted a dozen roses, the flowers of love, lying at her feet as a wretched testimonial of the state of her love life. A man she didn't love had just proposed marriage, and the man she did love was completely wrong for her. Her throat tightened, and her chin started to quiver uncontrollably.

Tears welled up, and she couldn't hold them back.

She sank to her knees in the middle of the living room floor and, surrounded by the broken flowers, covered her face with her hands and gave in to sobs that racked her entire body.

The doorbell rang, but she didn't answer it. She couldn't allow anyone to see her like this.

Mitchell's voice drifted through the door. "Carolyn? I know you're in there. Your car is in the driveway."

She didn't answer. She couldn't have spoken a word if she wanted to.

He knocked again. "Carolyn? Are you all right?"

When she still didn't answer, the doorknob rattled, then turned. The door slowly creaked open.

"Carolyn? The door was. . ." His voice drifted into silence.

Before she knew what was happening, she was pulled to her feet and locked solidly in a tight embrace, pressed against Mitchell from head to foot.

"What's wrong?" he murmured into her hair.

"It was Hank. He. . ." She couldn't finish.

His hands grasped her shoulders, and he pushed her away so he could look into her eyes. She turned her head so she didn't have to face him.

Mitchell's voice dropped to a low murmur, yet at the same time, it was very stern. "Did he hurt you?"

She shook her head, unable to stop the increased flow of tears or control the tremor in her voice. "N–no, n–nothing like that. H–he asked me to m–marry him."

In the blink of an eye, she was pressed into his chest again, but this time, instead of holding her by the shoulders, one of his large hands cupped the back of her head, gently pressing her cheek into his chest, the other hand pressed into the small of her back, and his chin rested on the top of her head.

With her ear pressed into the center of his chest, his voice sounded gruff and rumbly, and she could hear the rapid hammering of his heart. "And you said?"

She could barely choke the words out. "I said no. He didn't take it well."

His grip tightened, and he furthered the embrace by pushing his entire face into her hair. "Praise God. He's not right for you."

She shook her head, with her face still pressed into his chest, without answering.

He held her without speaking while she gained control, then released her when her sobs quieted. Carolyn excused herself to splash some cold water on her face and blow her nose.

She didn't want him to see her like this, but she also didn't want him to leave. Since no amount of makeup would erase the evidence of what happened, Carolyn stiffened her posture and entered the living room, where Mitchell was waiting for her. Instead of sitting on the couch, she found him standing with his back to her, studying her needlepoint. She didn't know if he really was that interested in it, but she appreciated him knowing she felt awkward about what she looked like. She also appreciated that the flowers were gone.

She sniffled one last time and sat on the couch. "What are you doing here? I wasn't expecting you." She purposely neglected mentioning that even though she wasn't expecting him, she had spent the earlier part of the day hoping he would show up.

"I had a few errands to do, and now that I'm done, I thought maybe we could spend the rest of the day together."

"I think I'll just stay home. Thanks for the thought, though."

He turned around but kept his distance. "I think it would be a good idea for you to get away for a while. It's Saturday afternoon. Why don't we go to a matinee? We can pick some weepy chick flick, and everyone will think you've been crying over the movie."

"A chick flick?"

"You know what I mean. One of those gushy movies where all the women sit there and cry through the movie, giving the guys a chance to put their arms around them and be macho."

Except for the putting his arms around her implication, it sounded perfect. For a while, she could get lost in the sad story of someone else's life and forget about the mess of her own life. She forced herself to smile. "I think that's a great idea."

"Good. While you were. . .uh, busy, I looked through the paper and found one. We have just enough time to get there if we hurry."

Mitchell yakked nonstop all the way to the theater, for which she was grateful. True to his plan, when the plot of the movie started getting weepy, he slipped his arm around her shoulders, which again started the flow of tears, allowing her the release she needed to get everything out of her system.

The whole time she cried, Mitchell merely sat there with his arm around her, every once in a while handing her another napkin to wipe her eyes and blow her nose. At the end of the movie, they remained seated until almost everyone left, then they slowly shuffled out.

"See. I knew you wouldn't be the only one crying. Just why do women cry at stuff like that?"

Carolyn blew her nose on the last napkin and shoved it into her purse. "I can't explain it."

He smiled and ran his thumb beneath her glasses, under her puffy eyes. "It was a rhetorical question. I think it's time to take you home. Wanna order pizza for supper?"

twelve

Mitchell sat at the kitchen table with the blue velvet pouch in his hand. With Jake gone and the dog asleep, the house was totally quiet, which gave him time to think before Carolyn arrived.

He couldn't count the times he'd tried to take her out for a quiet, romantic dinner, and each time something had happened or she'd managed to pick someplace not at all suitable to tell her what was in his heart and present her with the ring. Though often the activity was something fun—which in itself wasn't a bad thing—every time meant yet another delay and one more missed opportunity.

Again today, ideally they could have gone out for dinner. The competitor's strike had been averted, and not only did he not have to work overtime, he'd managed to get off early, which was a rare occurrence in itself. However, the rehearsal party was now only a few days away, and this was his last chance to practice what he needed to know before he had to do it for real, by himself.

Today was his last remedial cooking lesson, and Carolyn was due to arrive any minute.

It was less than the ideal situation, but if he didn't give Carolyn the ring today, he knew there wouldn't be a quiet day or time until all the cooking was done, the rehearsal party over with, and then after the big day on the weekend, the actual wedding. Following that, he would have to see Jake and Ellen off on their honeymoon, and then there would be the fallout with returning rented items and cleaning up. He didn't want to wait any longer.

He would give her the ring today. He tucked it into his pocket and patted it again.

Since the kitchen would be a mess when they were done, he'd prepared the living room as best he could. He'd vacuumed and dusted and done his best to pick as much dog hair off the couch as possible. For a romantic touch, he'd managed to find the one candle they owned and set it and a book of matches to the side, ready for the right moment.

Again, Mitchell pulled the pouch out of his pocket. He'd never thought much about jewelry before, but the little heart really was a perfect indication of his feelings for Carolyn. As delicately as he could, he plucked the tiny ring out of the bag and tipped it, making the small diamond sparkle in the light. He could see why such a ring would be called a promise ring. In a way, between the gold and the diamond, the ring resembled a miniature engagement ring. Hopefully, giving it to her could signify a promise of giving her a bigger diamond in the near future, along with the commitment of forever.

Both the kitchen and the living room were ready for Carolyn's arrival, but first, Mitchell needed to do one more thing. He tucked the ring back into the pouch, pulled the drawstring closed, dropped it back into his pocket, then folded his hands on the table and closed his eyes.

"Dear heavenly Father, thank You for bringing Carolyn into my life. She's exactly who I needed, and I pray that I am exactly who she needs as a perfect mate, designed and chosen by You. Again, I pray that tonight will present the perfect opportunity to give her this ring as a symbol of what our relationship could be and that You'll bless our time together. Amen."

At his closing amen, Killer started barking and ran for the door. Mitchell smiled and stood. God's timing was always perfect.

On his way through the living room, he could feel the pouch bouncing in his pocket. He craned his neck to look down at it and realized he could see its outline through the pocket of this particular shirt. Rather than run to his bedroom to put it in the drawer, he detoured a few steps and tucked it beside the lamp on the end table, where she wouldn't see it until the time was right.

She hadn't knocked yet, but that didn't stop him from opening the door to watch Carolyn as she walked up the sidewalk. The streetlights had come on, but the sky was still aglow with pink and purple, vivid with the beauty of God's creation and very fitting for Carolyn's arrival.

"Hi," he said, making no attempt to stop the wide smile he knew was on his face.

Carolyn tilted her head and narrowed one eye as she walked past him. "We are cooking today, aren't we?"

He couldn't stop smiling. "Of course."

She marched straight into his kitchen, and he trailed behind.

"I guess this is the last time I'll be helping you at home. Have you decided what you need help with today? I see you have a cookbook out. You told me you didn't own one."

He could feel his blush warming his cheeks, and he chided himself for it. "It's my mother's. The thing I really wanted to make was her specialty—crab snaps. Actually, that's why I took the course, to learn how to cook well enough to make them. No one believes that I can do this except Ellen. She knows I'm taking your classes."

Carolyn ran her finger down the recipe, mouthing the ingredients but not saying anything out loud. Her finger stopped moving when she got to the instructions. "This doesn't look too difficult. I don't see that you'll have a problem."

He didn't have to close his eyes to envision his first attempt at making his mother's famous crab snaps. It still made him shudder to think about it. "You have no idea."

They both checked the clock on the stove at the same time. "I guess we better get started." She ran her finger down the list again. "I'm going to assume you're using canned crab and not fresh?"

Mitchell groaned aloud. "I wasn't going to take the chance it was like shelling shrimp. Yes, it's canned."

"Okay, then go get the—"

The light flickered once, then went out.

Automatically, Mitchell walked to the wall switch and flicked it while Carolyn stared up at the dark fixture. "I don't believe this," he muttered under his breath.

Carolyn turned her head. "The living room looks awful dark. I don't think it's the bulb; I think the power just went out."

He strode to the window. The whole street was dark, as was his entire neighborhood and farther than he could see. "Houston, we have a problem," Mitchell mumbled and crossed his arms over his chest. He turned to Carolyn. "I don't have time for this. I have to learn how to make these things today. The party is Friday, only four days away."

He pulled open a drawer and grabbed a flashlight, then opened the phone directory. "I'm calling the electric company." A few moments later, he hung up and turned to Carolyn. "The recording said they're aware of an outage and a crew was being dispatched to determine the cause. There will be updates on the radio. I'll be right back."

Mitchell took the flashlight and retrieved his radio from the garage, where he used it when he was working on his car. He turned it on and tried to find a good station as he headed back to the kitchen.

"Do you keep everything you own in the garage?"

"Not everything I own fits in the pantry."

She sighed, then turned to study the stack of bowls and utensils he'd spread over the counters. "I don't know what to do. We could do this at my house, but by the time we get there, the power could be back on. Besides, all the ingredients are in your fridge, and I have a real aversion to opening the fridge when the power is out, just in case it doesn't come back for a long time."

Out of habit, Mitchell shone the flashlight on the battery-operated wall clock. "It's been out for twenty minutes already. I guess this serves me right for leaving the crab snaps until the last minute."

"Not really. Most of these things have to be prepared within a few days of the event. They get freezer burn quickly because of the individual-size portions. Besides, I doubt you have suitable storage containers."

He still had a couple of plastic containers he'd forgotten to give back to his mother the last time she sent him food, but other than that, whenever he had leftovers worth storing, he kept them in one of the two empty margarine containers he hadn't thrown out. Somehow he doubted Carolyn would consider those proper. He simply shrugged his shoulders, and her cute little sigh told him he was right in not replying.

"You shouldn't keep a seafood filling longer than overnight before serving. It would be best to make the pastries on Thursday, and then you could mix the filling and keep it in the fridge overnight and stuff them Friday before you have to go." She looked around the dark kitchen. "You really shouldn't prepare any of what you're going to serve until Wednesday or even Thursday. What else were you planning on making? Maybe we should go over your menu."

"I was going to make a few of the recipes we made in class and one of the things we did together. I really liked those rolled-up cheesy things that were dipped in the smashed-up nuts."

Carolyn sighed and crossed her arms over her chest. "Did I ever tell you that you have a unique way of describing these gourmet treats we've been making?"

"Many times. If we're not cooking, I guess we really don't need a lot of light." As if on cue, the beam of the flashlight faded, becoming slightly yellow. "It doesn't look like this battery is going to last much longer. I'd better get a candle."

He started toward the doorway when Carolyn's voice stopped him.

"Unlike your electric mixer, I can understand storing candles in the garage."

"Actually, I was going to the living room."

"I give up."

Mitchell soon returned to the kitchen. The smell of sulfur filled the air as he lit the candle and set it in the center of the table while Carolyn turned off the flashlight, which was almost dead anyway.

Carolyn pulled his mother's recipe book across the table. "What else were you going to make?"

He pulled up a chair and sat beside her. "Just the crab snaps. I wouldn't dare try to make anything else in there. I thought I'd stick to stuff I did in your class." He reached to the drawer behind him, grabbed the stack of handout sheets, and spread them over the table. "I know how to do these things, within reason. I was thinking I'd make the ones I liked best."

"You're just doing this now? You haven't decided on your menu or done your shopping yet?"

"I just bought what I needed to make the crab snaps because that's what I thought we were going to do today."

She grumbled something under her breath while she paged through the pile and pulled out the recipe he'd referred to earlier.

"Am I in trouble?"

"When did you expect to do this? Do you have a pen and paper?"

Mitchell found a pen, but he couldn't find an unused piece of paper in the dark, so he reached on top of the fridge and gave her the envelope from the phone bill. Her eyes narrowed as she accepted it from him, but she didn't say a word. He settled into the chair beside Carolyn and sat in silence as she skimmed the ingredients on the recipe he had selected and wrote out the shopping list in the flickering candlelight.

She slid the pile of paper back to him. "Which other ones do you want to make? And what did you do with the recipe for the dessert squares that I gave you?"

"It's in the pile somewhere."

Mitchell gave her his best smile, but it didn't ward off the annoyed sigh he knew was coming.

Together, they began the process of selecting the best choices for the party, and Carolyn dutifully added everything to the grocery list.

Instead of the romantic setting the candlelight was supposed to provide for the big moment he had planned, they now struggled to read by its questionable light; and instead of being receptive to him as he prepared to bare his soul, she was mad at him because he hadn't done his grocery shopping yet.

He couldn't believe how long the whole process took, nor could he believe that by the time she was finally adding the last of what they would need to the list, the power still hadn't come back on. The battery in his radio had expired during the wait.

Carolyn continued to write while he tried to think of a way to change the subject from cooking to how he felt about her when Killer ran to the door.

"I think your dog wants out."

"Killer would go to the back if she wanted out. She's at the front, and she's not barking, so that means Jake is home."

He heard Jake's voice before he saw him. "Wow. You should see the extent of this power failure. Did you know that it's dark all the way to. . ." His voice trailed off as he entered the kitchen. "Hello, Carolyn. It's nice to see you again."

She laid the pen down on the table. "Nice to see you, too, Jake."

Mitchell couldn't begrudge his friend's arrival. After all, Jake lived there, too. However, Jake's arrival had just disintegrated Mitchell's last hope of trying to have that private talk with Carolyn—unless the power failure was going to last a lot longer and they went to her house. "Did you have the radio on in the car? Any idea how much longer before the power comes back on?"

"They said about half an hour."

Carolyn stood. "That's too late to start, and it would take at least that long to pack up and move everything to my house."

Mitchell stood, as well. "What about grocery shopping? We can do that, now that we have a list."

"Sorry," Jake said. "Everything is out. They said on the radio that twenty-five thousand homes are without power."

Carolyn stepped toward the door. "Then I guess I'll be going."

Mitchell clenched his teeth and followed her to the door. Today, power failure or not, right moment or not, he could no longer wait. If he didn't give her the ring now, it would be another week before he could, and he didn't want to wait that long.

Since Jake's arrival meant no privacy inside, Mitchell followed her outside to her car parked on the dark street.

She reached for the handle, but before she opened the car door, Mitchell laid his hand on top of hers and gently pulled it to him.

"What are you doing?"

He massaged her wrist with his thumb. "I wanted to talk to you. I have to ask you something, and I don't know how to start."

Her smile made his heart flutter—something he thought only happened to women.

"It's okay. I know what you're going to say."

"You do?" He smiled back. That she had been thinking the same things was a positive and very encouraging sign about the growth of their relationship.

"Yes." She reached up with her other hand and gave his hand a tender squeeze. "I'm okay now. I'm not going to be seeing Hank anymore. It was a shock at the time, but I think I've known for a while that we weren't suited for each other. I'm sure that one day God will put the right man in my path. You're a good friend, Mitchell. I appreciate your concern."

"But—"

He let his hand go limp, and she moved away. "It's really late. I have to go home. The lack of electricity isn't going to prevent me from sleeping. Good night."

"Wait!" Out of habit, he reached up to his shirt pocket, but it was empty. He squeezed his eyes shut, remembering that he'd left the ring in the living room, ready for the right moment.

"I'll see you at class tomorrow."

Mitchell dropped his hand from his shirt pocket. "Yeah. Class tomorrow. Bye."

 за

Mitchell thunked his lunch pail on the counter and glanced at the clock, then at the calendar.

Today was Tuesday. Class night. It was also three days before the rehearsal party.

The power hadn't come on until after midnight Monday, when the only stores open were the convenience stores. He needed to start cooking as soon as he got home from work on Wednesday. That left tonight to do his shopping.

But tonight was cooking class. The last one he'd planned to take.

The clock on the wall ticked audibly.

He should have been shopping, not watching the clock.

Last night Carolyn called him a friend. She'd also said that one day God would put the right man in her path.

As far as he was concerned, God had put the right man in her path. She just didn't know it yet.

Mitchell grabbed his jacket and ran to his car. He didn't care if he was still at the grocery store at midnight when it closed, but he was going to class.

thirteen

"Okay, class, today we're going to make some classic hors d'oeuvres, starting with stuffed celery, and then some meat and vegetable combinations. First you need to—"

"Sorry I'm late. Excuse me."

Carolyn waited until Mitchell shuffled into the last empty chair, crossed his legs, and leaned back. All eyes settled on him, then slowly everyone returned their attention to the front.

She sighed and carried on with the lesson, but her mind was no longer fully on the food preparation. Today Mitchell should have been doing his shopping, since the power hadn't come back on in time to do it last night. She really hadn't expected to see him, and his presence in the class rattled her.

It had been difficult, but she'd come to a decision on what she was going to do about Mitchell. The times he had kissed her were seared into her memory for a lifetime. They didn't have a future together, but she couldn't stand the thought of never seeing him again. To keep whatever was happening between them as a platonic friendship was the best solution.

Yesterday she'd done her best to summon her courage and tell Mitchell indirectly that she considered him a friend. Mitchell was an intelligent person. She knew he would understand her meaning. It was only the shock of Hank's proposal that made her think she was in love with Mitchell, because the more she thought about it, the more she knew it wasn't possible. Mitchell was twenty-four years old. He'd started his first job right out of high school as a warehouse-man and worked his way into the dispatch office, where he now held a junior supervisory position. And he was happy with that.

She had to either continue to see him as a friend or not see him at all. She couldn't do that.

When the food preparations were done and all the creations eaten, Carolyn continued to walk from group to group, chatting and answering questions while everyone cleaned up. As usual, she arrived at Mitchell's group last.

Part of the routine she had set up was that every week the cleanup duties rotated, and today it was Mitchell's turn to wash dishes. He had his arms halfway to his elbows in the soapy water and his back was to her. She didn't mean to eavesdrop as she approached, but neither did she want to be rude and interrupt him.

"That's right. My best friend is marrying my sister, and I'm going to be cooking up all the food for the rehearsal party, which is Friday. I kind of backed myself into a corner. I took this course so I wouldn't have to eat crow."

Mrs. Finkleman started to chuckle. "That was a good thing. Crow would taste terrible." No one else laughed at her joke, but she didn't seem to notice.

Lorraine nearly dropped the pot she was returning to its place in the cupboard. "You're doing the cooking? You? The man who exploded an egg in the microwave trying to cook it faster?" She pointed her finger at him and burst out laughing.

"That was an accident," he mumbled while he scrubbed the last pan with far more force than necessary.

Carolyn gritted her teeth at Lorraine's barb and stepped into their little circle. "Everyone makes mistakes, especially when they're still learning. Mitchell is going to do just fine."

All noise and action immediately ceased, not only in Mitchell's group, but also the two neighboring groups. When the other two groups noticed the silence, they also suddenly quieted. All eyes turned to her.

Carolyn stiffened and made eye contact with everyone except Mitchell as she spoke. "Next week is our last class, and we're going to make a few dessert items. I look forward to seeing you all then. Good night, everyone."

She didn't wait for a reply, but turned and headed for her demonstration table to tidy her own mess as the ladies began to filter out.

As usual, Mitchell was the last person besides her remaining in the room. This time, she really didn't want to talk to him. She'd made a public display of defending him when he was perfectly capable of defending himself.

Also as usual, he appeared at her side before she was finished cleaning.

"I need to talk to you."

He continued before she could protest.

"I have something for you, and this isn't exactly the way I wanted to give it to you, but I'm going to do it anyway." He patted his pockets until he found what he was looking for, pulled out a little blue velvet jewelry pouch, then handed it to her without a word.

She took the pouch from him but didn't check inside. "How did you know it was my birthday tomorrow?"

He hesitated but recovered quickly. "I didn't know it was your birthday tomorrow. If that's the case, then I'm going to have to figure out something special to give you to mark the occasion. This," he said, pointing at the pouch, "has nothing to do with your birthday. Quite honestly, I've been meaning to give this to you for a while and never got the chance."

Her heart started pounding, and she broke into a sweat.

Her hands trembled as she opened it.

When she saw what was inside, she couldn't keep the tremor from her voice. "It's a ring."

It was small and delicate and beautiful. A small, sparkling diamond in the middle of a gold heart glittered in the fluorescent light.

He scooted around the table and was beside her before she realized he had moved. "Try it on."

Her hands shook so much, she was afraid she would drop it. Very slowly, she slipped it on. It was a little too big for her ring finger so she changed it to her middle finger, which seemed to minimize its statement. A promise ring.

"I don't know what to say. Why are you doing this?"

He smiled that lopsided smile she was getting to know so well. When his dimple appeared, her throat went dry. "I'm courting you, Carolyn. Can't you tell? If you can't, I must be doing something wrong."

He had done nothing wrong, but until now, she had done a fine job of convincing herself that his constant appearances and the warm fuzzies she felt in his presence meant only friendship.

"Don't you remember that, as of tomorrow, I'm nine years older than you? You can't court me. It's not right."

"Age doesn't matter, Carolyn. At least it doesn't matter to me. You're the special person you are regardless of your age or mine. We share lots of common interests, and we share a common faith. Nothing else matters."

"I think it's a little more complicated than that." She still wasn't sure they had common interests, although they did enjoy their time together. While she'd always heard that opposites attract, she had a feeling she and Mitchell were too opposite for consideration. He was nothing like the man she had prayed for as her perfect mate. She almost shuddered visibly as she imagined Mitchell with all Hank's sensible and mature character traits. She didn't want another Hank. But Mitchell wasn't right for her, either.

While finding a woman with a strong faith in Christ seemed very important to Mitchell, she couldn't see that she could ever be the fun-loving and active woman he needed. Ten years ago she had tried skiing, hiking, and other more strenuous activities. Not that she was anywhere near a couch potato, but about the time she turned thirty, her interests turned to quieter and less demanding leisure pursuits.

"I don't know if I can accept this. I don't think this is such a good idea."

He picked up her hands, then rubbed his thumb over the small ring on her finger. "The saleslady said it was a promise ring, and I am making a promise to you, Carolyn. But if you want to, we can start off slowly and call it a friendship ring."

"But it's a heart. Hearts don't mean friendship."

His hand rose to her cheek. Her eyes drifted shut as he brushed her skin with the backs of his fingers. "Then think of it however you want. All I want is for you to keep an open heart because I 1–1–1. . . I like you a lot."

Footsteps echoed in the hall, drawing their attention to Mr. O'Sullivan checking the classrooms to make sure everyone had left the building for the night. No doubt he'd noticed that hers was the only car left in the staff parking lot and was dutifully checking on her.

She cleared her throat and opened her eyes, resisting as hard as she could not to lean her head into his fingers. "I think it's time to go home."

"I can't go home yet. I have to go grocery shopping."

"Pardon me?"

"I have to start cooking as soon as I get home from work tomorrow, so I'm going shopping tonight. The mega store is open until midnight, so I'll have just enough time. Wanna come?"

ও

Carolyn sent her high school students to the kitchenettes to do their projects, then walked from group to group to supervise and assist.

Every time she moved her hand, she became aware of the unaccustomed ring on her finger. She'd never worn a ring before; no one had ever given her one. She enjoyed and appreciated both the look and the feel of the fine gold and tiny diamond on her finger, but conversely, it was a constant reminder of Mitchell.

She still didn't know what to do about him. A man didn't give a woman a ring with a heart on it to signify friendship.

The man was courting her. Part of her wanted it, and part of her said it wouldn't work.

A loud bang accompanied by teenaged laughter drew

Carolyn's attention back to her class. Group three again needed more help than the rest of the class, so she stopped thinking about Mitchell and began showing her students how to properly separate an egg when the sound of footsteps clicked on the tile floor so loudly, it almost sounded like someone was wearing taps on their shoes.

"That's Miss Rutherford," a teen's voice piped up.

Abruptly, Carolyn turned to see a man in a horridly bright red bellhop uniform overly embellished with glossy black stripes down the sides of the legs and arms. The outfit was topped off with the ugliest hat she'd ever seen, and the man was holding a brightly wrapped parcel in one hand. He blew a tuning harmonica, then ceremoniously cleared his throat.

"Happy birthday to you," he sang, drawing out the familiar refrain.

Most of the students burst out laughing.

Carolyn thought she'd die. But she would kill Mitchell first. Except that would probably be a sin.

Red-faced and stiff as a board, she listened to the badly dramatized rendition wishing her a happy birthday. When the last torturous line was sufficiently drawn out, with a tip of his fez, the man offered her the gift. The class gave him a rousing round of applause to which he bowed with a flourish and left amidst another chorus of catcalls and whistles.

Carolyn continued to stare at the vacant doorway, barely aware of the brightly wrapped box in her hands. She couldn't believe the school secretary had allowed him in.

Another round of applause and cheers from the students snapped her mind back to what she was supposed to have been doing.

Carolyn cleared her throat. "That's enough nonsense. Let's finish up before we run out of time."

"What did you get?"

"How old are you?"

"Who sent the singing telegram? Your boyfriend?"

Most of the teenaged girls giggled.

Carolyn sighed. She didn't exactly think of Mitchell as her boyfriend, but the trouble was, she didn't know what to call him. The only thing she did know was that of all her friends, only Mitchell would do such a thing as send a singing telegram.

Again, her fingers drifted to touch the tiny promise ring, outlining the shape of the heart without looking at it. Certainly they'd gone beyond mere friendship, but she still hadn't figured out to what. In order to get the focus off her personal life and back to the home economics class she was supposed to be leading, she had to provide a response. "Yes, my boyfriend."

"Ooh," the students chorused.

"That's enough, class. Now get back to your kitchenettes."

Slowly, everyone shuffled back to their lesson project of the day, although she both saw and heard little whisperings in every group.

By the time the lunch bell rang, she was more than ready to be left alone. Rather than go to the staff room, Carolyn sat at her desk and stared at the brightly colored box. It was not professionally wrapped. The paper was cut crooked and the bow lay off center. Only Mitchell could have wrapped this.

Slowly, Carolyn picked off the brightly colored bow and stuck it to the side of her penholder. She unhitched the tape and pulled off the paper.

The box was from a specialty chocolate store, and inside was an assortment of foil-wrapped chocolate kisses and a small card filled with scrawling handwriting.

Happy birthday, Carolyn.
One sweet kiss for each sweet year. Enjoy them, and think of me.

Love, Mitchell

Carolyn squeezed her eyes shut and sighed.

She didn't know how to respond. As strange as it was, the gesture was unique and far more personal than any gift she had ever received. The addition of the chocolates made the whole thing rather romantic, in a Mitchell Farris kind of way.

She picked up the note and studied it. His handwriting was atrocious, but as bad as it was, the signature "Love, Mitchell" jumped off the paper at her.

She didn't want to think about the ramifications of the chocolate kisses.

Rather than dwell on it any longer, Carolyn popped one into her mouth, reread the note, and counted the chocolate morsels while the one melted in her mouth. To her dismay, the store had made a mistake, because, counting the one already in her mouth, there were only thirty-two.

She carefully closed the box, mentally kicking herself for having a chocolate before she ate her lunch, and tucked the box into her desk drawer. She checked the clock, picked up her purse, retrieved her lunch bag from the large fridge, and made her way to the staff lunch room, where she could phone Mitchell to thank him for a very unusual but very special birthday gift.

The second she opened the door, a chorus of "happy birthdays" greeted her, along with a cake with one large lighted candle. Carolyn clutched her purse tightly so she wouldn't drop it or her lunch. All the other teachers either cheered or laughed at her surprise.

Carolyn's eyes burned, but she blinked a few times, lifted her glasses, and wiped tears away. "Th–thank you," she stammered. In the six years she'd worked at the school, no one had ever acknowledged her birthday. Though the date was on her job application, she'd never told anyone. Of course some of them would have known because of the singing telegram, but she hadn't expected this.

Karen, the secretary, stood. "Come on, Carolyn. Blow out the candle before it burns the cake down or sets off the smoke alarm."

She sucked in a deep breath, blew out the candle, and everyone applauded.

Karen stepped forward, pulled the candle out of the cake,

then hurried to run the smoking wick under the cold water. "Your boyfriend phoned first thing this morning and asked for permission and the best time to send the singing telegram, otherwise, I wouldn't have known it was your birthday. You should have said something." Karen placed a stack of paper plates and a knife beside the cake. "Here—we got you a card. Happy birthday."

Carolyn lowered her head. "Thank you," she mumbled as she tore the flap open. Everyone had signed it and added a silly comment.

Conversations that had ended when she walked in restarted, and soon it was just like any other lunch break. As everyone finished eating, Carolyn cut a piece of cake for each teacher. She'd barely finished her own slice when the bell rang to return to the classrooms, not allowing her the time to phone Mitchell.

The students all wished her a happy birthday as they filed in. Carolyn forced herself to smile and thank them all, knowing that the singing telegram had now become hot news throughout the entire school population during the lunch break. It also gave her a horrible premonition that there would be a picture of the young man and a summary of the incident in the school's yearbook.

The afternoon seemed the longest in the time since she'd begun her teaching career. By the time the bell rang signaling the close of classes, she was eager to go home.

She hurried to tidy her demonstration area and was almost finished checking all the kitchenettes to make sure everything was in order for the first class the next day when footsteps echoed through the door opening.

"Hi," a familiar deep voice drawled. "Happy birthday."

Carolyn spun around, her hand pressed to her heart. "Mitchell! What are you doing here? Why aren't you at work?"

"I have lots of time coming to me, so I took off early for a change." He grinned that same grin she'd come to know and love, and her heart pounded even more. "I brought you something."

"But you already gave me a wonderful birthday present. Thank you very much. It was really different."

He dangled something shiny in the air. "I brought you the last kiss."

She couldn't hold back her smile. The store hadn't made a mistake. "That's very sweet, but you didn't have to take time off and come all this way just for that." As she spoke, she walked toward him to collect it.

No sooner had she taken her first step than Mitchell hastily unwrapped the kiss and popped it into his mouth.

"Hey! That was mine!"

She watched as he guiltlessly grinned, chewed it, and swallowed. "Nope. That one was for me." He stepped forward. "This one's for you."

Before she realized what he was doing, he wrapped his arms around her and kissed her. And without thinking about it, she kissed him back. The combination of his embrace and the scent of chocolate on his breath made her head spin and her already pounding heart jump into overdrive.

The bang of someone slamming a locker in the hallway caused them both to jump. Mitchell released her and backed up a step, his confusion evident in his expression.

"I didn't mean for this to happen like that," he stammered, then shook his head. "No, that's wrong. Yes, I did mean for that to happen. But not here."

If he suggested they go elsewhere and pick up where they left off, she thought she might run screaming for the hills.

"I had to come here to see you because it's Bible study night, and I know we said we'd go to mine tonight, but I'm going to have to get a rain check until next week. I'm going to start making the food for Friday tonight. Knowing my luck, something will happen, and I'll need two full evenings to do this. I hope you're proud of me for planning ahead."

She smiled. "Yes. I'm proud of you. If you need help, I can skip this one week."

He pressed one palm to his heart. "You're asking if I need

help? You mean you actually considered that I could do this all by myself, without help?"

"Do you want me to be honest or make you feel good?"

His little grin made her breath catch. "I won't back you into a corner and make you answer that. Instead, I have an idea. How about if we pick up a couple of burgers, and I'd be forever grateful if you could join me in the kitchen this evening, just in case I need you."

There was no "just in case" to consider. "Yes, I think I'll do that."

fourteen

Carolyn opened the bag and slid the hamburger and large order of fries across the kitchen table, keeping the other hamburger and smaller order of fries for herself while Mitchell started a pot of coffee.

Killer lay in her bed in the corner of the kitchen, ignoring them while they prayed over the food.

"I've been meaning to ask you why you call that sweet animal Killer. That has to be the gentlest, most unexcitable dog I've ever seen."

Mitchell's ears reddened. "It was one of my lesser inspired moments. I thought if the dog was such a marshmallow, a name like Killer might preserve her reputation, but everyone just laughs."

"Is she so calm because she's old, or is she going deaf?"

"I'm not sure. I guess she's about five or so. I know she's not deaf. She appears the split second I open the cupboard where her dog cookies are."

"You guess? You mean you don't know how old your dog is?"

"Not really. We got her from the pound. Jake and I were looking for a watchdog because we'd just been robbed. We were looking at a bigger dog, but when we learned Killer was going to be put down, those big, sad eyes got to me, and I took her. We haven't been robbed since, so I suppose she's at least partly responsible for that. She's friendly, anyway. And she doesn't annoy the neighbors with tons of barking."

"That was a sweet thing to do!"

"Don't go getting gushy on me. It's just a dog."

She wanted to hug him just for being nice but didn't dare after what happened at the school.

As soon as they finished eating, Mitchell bundled the paper

136

wrappings and they set to work. As a matter of pride, he insisted on doing the pastry while Carolyn mixed the fillings and pâté. Together, they shaped cheese balls and rolled them in the chopped nuts.

Killer jumped to her feet and ran to the door. She barked once, then sat quietly and wagged her tail.

Mitchell wiped his hands on his pants, leaving floury hand-prints on his thighs, and headed for the door. "Killer barked, so it's not Jake. I'm not expecting anyone."

Carolyn stood in the kitchen doorway, watching.

Before Mitchell got to the door, it opened and Jake walked in, followed by Gordie and Roland.

"Mitch? What are you doing here? It's your Bible study night." Jake glanced at the flour on Mitchell's nose and burst out laughing.

Gordie stepped forward. "Hi, Miss Rutherford."

Carolyn cringed. Miss Rutherford. Is that what she would be to his friends? Not his companion or his girlfriend, but the teacher, Miss Rutherford? She smiled shakily. "Hi, Gordie," she mumbled.

Mitchell's posture stiffened as he faced his friend. "We're not in school anymore. Her name is Carolyn."

"Oops. Sorry, Miss—er, Carolyn."

Mitchell turned his back on his friends and moved to Carolyn's side. "We're busy here. Couldn't you go to the cof-fee shop?"

Jake ignored Mitchell's question. He crossed his arms over his chest and craned his neck in an attempt to see over Mitchell's shoulder into the kitchen. "What are you making?"

Mitchell turned his back on his friends and grabbed her hand. "It's a surprise," he grumbled. "Come on, Carolyn, let's finish up."

Unfortunately, Mitchell's friends trailed behind. They stood beside the table and gaped at the rows of hors d'oeuvres neatly set into the storage containers Carolyn had brought. Jake picked up a finished cheese ball and popped it into his mouth.

Roland stepped forward. "If you can have one, so can I." He followed Jake's example and snitched a cheese ball. Gordie took only a second to follow suit.

"Wow," Gordie mumbled. "Forget the wedding. All the good food's going to be at the rehearsal party."

Jake swept his hand in the air over the tray of goodies. "Did you really do this by yourself? Carolyn did it, and you've been watching, right?"

Mitchell raised one finger in the air and opened his mouth, but Jake interrupted him. "No, forget I asked. I can tell by the look of you that you've been doing more than watching. I wouldn't have believed it if I hadn't seen it with my own eyes. And there isn't a wiener in any of this."

Carolyn bit her lip. She had done some of the more difficult steps for him, but Mitchell really had worked hard, both in class and now, and he really had put what he learned into practice.

Jake pointed at the pastry shapes Mitchell had been in the middle of shaping when his friends had arrived. "What are those things?"

"Those things," Mitchell said as he crossed his arms and tapped one foot, "are going to be the pastry shells for the crab snaps."

"Well, what do ya know."

Roland pointed to the counter. "What are you doing with that bag of mushrooms? Making little teeny-weeny pizzas? Where's the pepperoni?"

"I'm making stuffed mushroom caps."

The three of them stood in one spot, staring at the bag of mushrooms as if it were some object from outer space.

Gordie shook his head. "Stuffed mushrooms? You? You've gotta be kidding."

"That does it," Mitchell muttered. "Get lost." Following his words, Mitchell practically shoved them out of the kitchen. "I wish kitchens had doors you could lock," he mumbled.

Carolyn grinned. "I think you should take it as a compliment."

He uttered something unintelligible in return.

The sounds of Jake and Gordie and Roland making themselves comfortable drifted from the living room. Killer returned to her bed in the corner of the kitchen and fell back to sleep, and she and Mitchell continued with their cooking. Jake reappeared in the kitchen to help himself to the coffee they'd made earlier, then returned for a second cup, and not long after that he came back to make another pot. Considering the time it took him with every return trip, it gave Carolyn a sneaking suspicion that he was doing more than tending to the coffee. Jake was doing some serious looting.

After Jake's fourth trip into the kitchen, it finally dawned on Mitchell that his friend was pilfering the food. Carolyn struggled to stifle her laughter as Mitchell almost physically threw his best friend out of the kitchen, threatening Jake's life if he dared to return.

When they were done, Mitchell washed his hands in the kitchen sink with the dish detergent, and they carefully snapped the covers onto the containers.

Carolyn counted everything. "We did really well today. We only have a few things left to do tomorrow."

"Don't speak too soon. Since Jake seems to like these so much, I think it would all be safer if you took it home. Do you have room in your fridge until Friday? I know it's a lot to ask, but even the Bible says to remove temptation. I really don't think Ellen would be very pleased with me if her future husband showed up with a black eye on their wedding day."

"No problem. I can take most of this home." She picked up the remaining recipe sheets. "You don't even need to get off early tomorrow since there's only a few things left to do."

His triumphant smile would have made a winning toothpaste commercial. "Yeah. We did great."

"Since your mom still has the cast on her arm, who is going to put everything out and stuff and bake the crab snaps on Friday?"

"I am."

"Do you have any idea how long that's going to take?"

He shook his head. "I hadn't really thought about it."

"You've proved my point. You've prepared the food, but you're the best man. You should be with the rest of the wedding party, not spending all your time in the kitchen. If you want, while everyone is at the church, I could get the food ready if your parents wouldn't mind me being in their house when they're not home."

"No. I want you to come to the party as my guest, not the hired help."

"I don't mind. I could be both."

"I probably don't have a lot of choice, do I?"

"Not really. Someone has to do it."

"I won't let you do all the work. I made this stuff. I want to serve it."

"I'm sure you'll have plenty of opportunity. Now I think it's time for me to go."

He checked his wristwatch, then glanced at the clock on the stove. "I'll help you carry this to your car."

Once everything was stacked securely, Mitchell stood in such a spot that she couldn't open the car door without hitting him with it.

"I'm really sorry that I didn't take you out for dinner on your birthday. You shouldn't have been working on your special day, but I was desperate."

"It's okay. I enjoy making things in the kitchen. Besides, the singing telegram more than made up for it. It was a birthday I'll never forget." Even more memorable than the young man in the horrid costume was the last of the kisses, but she wasn't going to admit that to him.

"Have I told you how much I appreciate your help?"

"A few dozen times, yes."

He grinned. "Then have I told you how much I'm looking forward to tomorrow, when we'll be finishing this up?"

"I believe so."

"Did I tell you that I can hardly wait until the rehearsal

party, where I can show you off not only as the person responsible for teaching me how to make all this stuff, but also as my date?"

She wasn't sure he'd emphasized the part about being his date, although his meaning when he talked about it had been clear enough, so she nodded.

"Well, then, have I told you how much I love you?"

She opened her mouth, but no words came out.

Quickly, Mitchell stepped forward, tipped her chin up with his index finger, and brushed a light kiss to her lips. "Good night, Carolyn. Drive safely. I'll see you tomorrow."

As quickly as he had moved forward, he stepped back and opened the door for her.

"Good night, Mitchell," she mumbled as she scrambled behind the wheel and took off.

She obviously drove home, but Carolyn found herself standing in her kitchen loading the food they'd made into her fridge, remembering nothing of the drive. She only remembered Mitchell's words.

He loved her. She loved him, too, but that didn't make the relationship right or good. She couldn't believe Mitchell didn't see how wrong they were for each other.

For now, they had the excitement of a new relationship, but when everything faded to everyday routine, he wouldn't find her so interesting, especially when age started to creep up on her faster than it would creep up on him. Projecting further, she tried to imagine what it would be like when she was sixty-five, ready to retire, and wanting to travel and Mitchell was still fifty-six, with many more years of active employment ahead of him. By the time he reached sixty-five, she would be nearly seventy-four. She wasn't likely to be able to keep up with him then.

But for now, she wanted to have children and to do so before she was thirty-five. Her prospective mate had to be ready for an almost-instant family. While twenty-four was certainly not too young to be a responsible father, she didn't know if Mitchell wanted children. And if he did, she didn't know if he wanted them right away. She didn't even know if to him love meant getting married versus simply having a steady relationship.

Love was more complicated than a case of the warm fuzzies. She needed security, compatibility, and strength. But most of all, she needed to seek God's will for the man she saw as His choice for her.

She didn't want to think about Hank and his proposal. One thing she was sure of was that God wanted her to be happy.

Despite the late time, she knew she would never sleep. Instead, Carolyn picked up her Bible and turned to 1 Corinthians 13 and read all the things God said about love. Patience. Kindness. Not envious or boastful. Humble. She read the section a dozen times, and to the best of her knowledge, Mitchell was all of those things.

She didn't know what to do, so she buried her face in her hands and prayed for a sign that a relationship with Mitchell Farris was God's will for her.

❧

Carolyn helped Mitchell stack the containers of food into the back of his car, and they began the journey to his parents' house.

Today was the day.

She'd never been so nervous in her life.

It hadn't occurred to her until this moment that she hadn't considered the other members of the wedding party who would be there today—the bride's friends, or worse, Mitchell's family.

Realistically, she could expect Mitchell's sister to be at least one year younger than Mitchell. She would be participating in a social function with people who could possibly be her former students. She wouldn't be Carolyn, an acquaintance or possible friend. She'd be Miss Rutherford, the teacher from their high school days. As their teacher and person in a position of authority, she was careful to define the line between the generations. Except for helping the odd student with extra lessons, she kept her private life exactly that, private.

The name Ellen Farris wasn't immediately familiar, although she could hardly be expected to remember every student who passed through her class year after year. But even if she hadn't had Mitchell's sister as one of her students, the possibility existed that she had taught a few of the bridesmaids, some of whom would be friends of Ellen's from high school. She didn't want to think of the other guests at the wedding. Not that she'd never bumped into a former student at a social function, but this time it would be different because she would be accompanying Mitchell as a peer rather than an instructor.

Trying to be as discreet as possible, she glanced at herself in the rearview mirror to see if she looked her age, and she did. The beginnings of crow's-feet and other telltale signs of being over thirty couldn't be hidden, and since she rarely used anything more than a touch of eye shadow and lipstick, if she suddenly put on makeup to hide her age, it would only look worse.

"We're almost there."

Carolyn blinked and started paying attention to where they were. They had traveled about ten minutes and neither of them had spoken, which she found odd because Mitchell tended to be chatty in the car.

Upon the arrival of the wedding party, Mitchell planned to introduce her to everyone she hadn't met, and then everyone would leave except Carolyn. Then, once she was alone, she would start setting out the food and make the punch and put everything that required heating in the oven. Since the rehearsal itself wouldn't be long, she would have barely enough time to get everything done before the wedding party returned, and then it would be time to eat.

"Are you as nervous as I am?" she asked as she smoothed a few imaginary wrinkles from her sleeve.

Mitchell slowed the car, and they pulled into the driveway of a large white house with blue painted trim and a cheery flower garden in front.

He killed the engine but made no move to exit the car. He remained seated, rested one arm across the back of his seat as he turned the upper half of his body to her, and gripped the top of the steering wheel tightly with his left hand. "Before we go in, there's something I neglected to tell you. I've been afraid to mention it, but I think you should know this before you meet my parents."

Her stomach sank. She swallowed hard and listened.

"My mom and dad were only sixteen when she got pregnant. They got married when I was three. They became Christians when I was in kindergarten."

She waited in silence, but he didn't say anything more. "Why are you telling me this?"

He stiffened and grasped her hands as he spoke, holding them firmly enough that it would be an effort to pull away from him. The tightness in her stomach worsened her fear of what he was going to say.

"Just so you'll be prepared when you see them. I should have told you sooner, but I didn't know how. I'm sorry."

She stared at Mitchell, trying to picture an older version of him, which wasn't difficult, because she'd often tried to fantasize him into being older.

"It's okay," she said, still not sure she understood why he thought the state of his parents' early relationship was her concern. They were Christians now and had been for years, which was all that mattered.

Mitchell straightened and tugged at his shirt collar, then ran his hands down his sleeves, straightening out the wrinkled fabric. "We'd better get moving. We have to get all the food inside and some of the work done before everyone gets here."

Walking side by side, they approached the house. Instead of knocking and waiting, Mitchell rang the doorbell and opened the door. He poked his head inside, calling out that they had arrived, walked in, and shut the door behind them.

A couple approached from the stairs. The woman was blond, tall, thin, and absolutely beautiful. She wore fashionably snug jeans along with a loose, short-sleeved, cotton pullover sweater. Her right arm was bound in a cast, which was supported by a sling.

The man was about the same height as Mitchell and just as attractive in a different sort of way because of the maturity that enriched his handsome features. He smiled a greeting that would have melted any woman's heart. He carried himself with a combination of good looks and confident manners that gave him a timeless appeal, except he wasn't old enough to need to be timeless. He was drop-dead gorgeous. It took a few seconds for it to fully sink in that this chic couple was Mitchell's mother and father.

The resemblance between father and son was striking, and he sported a physique identical to his son's. They almost could have been brothers, except for the fact that since Mitchell's mother was standing beside him, Carolyn could see some of her features in Mitchell.

"Carolyn, these are my parents, Kim and Roger. Mom, Dad, this is Carolyn."

Carolyn blinked, speechless. In a single instant, she understood the meaning of Mitchell's attempt to caution her about meeting his parents. She had friends the same age as Mitchell's mother, but that wasn't what hit her the hardest. Doing some quick math, she calculated that Roger was forty years old, only one year older than Hank—and closer to her age than Mitchell was by two years.

Carolyn felt sick.

His mother smiled. "So you're Mitchell's friend, the cooking teacher. We've heard so much about you. I'm so pleased to finally meet you." With her arm in the cast, she awkwardly glanced down while Mitchell's father extended his hand. Carolyn responded with the limpest handshake of her life.

"Yes, pleased to meet you, Carolyn."

The second his father released her hand, Mitchell slipped his around her waist and gave her a little squeeze, drawing both his parents' gazes to the obvious show of affection. His mother's eyebrows rose, but no comment was made. Carolyn should have parroted the usual polite reply, but for a moment she couldn't have formed words if her life depended on it. She didn't know how to address them. She had called Hank's parents by Mr. and Mrs. and besides, they were. . .older. If they were at school, she would have addressed a student's parents as Mr. and Mrs., regardless of the age difference, but in any other social situation, she would have greeted them using their first names.

In this case, she settled for, "Thank you. It's good to meet you, too."

Mitchell's mother cleared her throat. "Ellen and Jake phoned to say they're going straight to the church. We should get moving, too, or we're going to be late. While Roger and Mitchell empty the car, I'll show you the kitchen and where everything is, and then we'll be off." Carolyn followed Kim into the kitchen, but every word of explanation and directions went in one ear and out the other. Not only was Mitchell's mother a talented cook, she was gorgeous and slim. Carolyn wondered if her hair would go gray before Kim's did.

Thankfully, his parents left the house quickly, but Mitchell lingered.

"Are you okay?"

She wasn't, but she didn't know what to say. She nodded dumbly.

"We'll talk about it later." Before she could think or move, his fingers tipped her chin up, and he gave her a light, lingering kiss. Very gently, he stroked her cheek with his fingertips, tilted his head, and brushed one more light kiss to her lips. The sweetness of his actions nearly made her cry.

He spoke so softly, she could barely hear. "Remember, I love you."

Before she could collect her thoughts enough to respond, he turned and sprinted down the sidewalk, hopped into his car, and drove off.

Carolyn busied herself setting out the food on plates and

preparing what needed to go in the oven. She didn't want to think about Mitchell, and she especially didn't want to think about his father. Instead, she paid an inordinate amount of attention to the exact amount of filling needed for each individual crab snap, and then put all her concentration on rearranging everything to make the most attractive display of all the food Mitchell had made.

fifteen

Mitchell smiled politely at a joke that had the rest of the wedding party nearly rolling in the aisles with laughter. He stood where he was supposed to stand and waited while the pastor instructed everyone on exactly what to do and how to walk.

She never said she loved him back. The first time he'd said it casually, just dropping it into the conversation, but he'd never been so nervous in his life. He didn't know how she would respond, so he left her an opportunity to bolt, and she had. This time hadn't been much different except that he was the one who ran, using the excuse that everyone was waiting for him. But before he took off, he had hesitated. He'd seen the shock on her face.

Ever since the first time he met Hank, Mitchell had worried about how Carolyn would react to meeting his parents, especially his father. At the time it had hit him right in the gut to see how much older Hank was than Carolyn. It had been almost like looking at his father, and it shook him.

It had taken him a long time to deal with the fact that his parents had been unmarried teenagers when he was born. Both his parents had continued with their schooling, except that his mother had taken a year off and graduated one year later. His grandparents, whom he loved dearly, had helped and supported them until his parents graduated, got jobs, and married.

His family had struggled, but now, twenty-four years later, his parents were happily married and in a few years would be celebrating their silver anniversary. Ellen had been born a year after his parents were married, after they had become Christians. Their story had a happy ending, unlike the story of so many teenage pregnancies.

As much as his friends had always been impressed with his

youthful mother and father, Carolyn was having exactly the opposite reaction, and he couldn't blame her. He should have found a way to mention it earlier so it didn't come as such a shock.

Mitchell turned his head and stared blankly at the wall, ignoring the noise and clamor around him. He could only imagine Carolyn's misgivings about getting involved in a relationship with a man whose parents were only seven years older than she was.

Mitchell buried his hands in his pockets and continued to stare at the wall. He desperately loved Carolyn with all his heart and soul, but now there was nothing he could do. He had to leave it in God's hands and trust that if this was the woman God wanted him to have, then it would be so. If not, he would have to let her go.

He pulled his hands out of his pockets, stood the way he'd been told, and turned around to watch Ellen's friends walking down the aisle one at a time. Today they were all wearing jeans, but on Saturday they'd be in long dresses.

He looked at Jake, who was now standing beside him. Jake's hands were shaking as he watched the proceedings. For now, Jake rammed his hands into his pockets and grinned like an idiot trying to appear unaffected, but Mitchell wasn't fooled.

Mitchell thought back to when Jake announced his and Ellen's engagement. After he'd gotten over the shock that his best friend really was going to marry his sister, Mitchell had teased Jake about getting tied down and having to answer to someone else for almost everything he did.

Mitchell now knew differently. Jake was happy. He had the commitment, companionship, and love of a woman for the rest of his life—if he didn't do anything foolish enough to break that trust. Mitchell wanted the same.

He wanted to be Carolyn's soul mate for the rest of their lives. When he gave her the promise ring and then kissed her at the school, he hoped that she could love him and see a future with him.

Now, he wasn't so sure.

From the change in Jake's expression, Mitchell could tell it was Ellen's turn to walk up the aisle. As she hung on to their father's arm, Ellen was grinning from ear to ear, staring at Jake.

Jake was smiling, but his eyes were getting glassy, and even though it wasn't very macho, Mitchell envied his friend. He also wondered what it would be like on Saturday when everyone was all dressed up, the wedding march was playing, and everything was for real.

Once Ellen arrived at the front, the pastor talked to Jake and Ellen about their vows, exchanging rings, and signing the marriage certificate. When the pastor announced Jake would then kiss the bride, Jake grabbed Ellen around the waist and bent her backward. Ellen squealed in surprise and grabbed Jake's shoulders, and Jake kissed her fully while everyone else hooted and cheered.

Mitchell wanted to kiss Carolyn like that—willingly, before friends and family and before God.

When Jake and Ellen finally separated, the pastor directed the wedding party to pair up and exit the sanctuary as they would when the ceremony was over. As best man, he stepped out before the other attendants and escorted Melissa down the aisle immediately following Jake and Ellen.

Once they all stood in the lobby, the official rehearsal was finally over.

He wanted to be the first one back at the house to see Carolyn, but he had to wait while his mother talked to the pastor. He stood impatiently by the door, and soon his dad joined him.

"My baby girl is getting married tomorrow."

"Yeah." Mitchell wished his father's son was getting married, too, although the more he thought about it, the less likely it seemed that it would happen.

"That sure was nice of your friend to offer to help you with the food instead of hiring a caterer. We'll have to think of some way to thank her."

His friend. He wanted Carolyn to be more than just his friend. "Yeah, we should do that."

"I could be mistaken, but you appear to think of Carolyn as more than a friend."

Mitchell stared at his father. He figured it was a little late in his upbringing to be talking about the women he dated.

"How old is she, Mitch?"

"She's only thirty-three." Mitchell turned to his father, daring him to say anything more about Carolyn's age. He wanted to defend her, to justify to his father that it was okay for him to be dating an older woman and that Carolyn was more suited to him than any woman he'd ever met in his life.

"Is she a Christian?"

"Yes."

"You're in love with her, aren't you?"

"Yes, I am."

"Then I guess that's all that matters. I wish you God's blessings, Mitch."

Mitchell rammed his hands into his pockets and stared blankly out the window. "I don't know how she feels about me. The difference in our ages bothers her."

His father nodded and rubbed his chin with his index finger and thumb. "I've seen a few couples where the woman is three or four years older, but it doesn't usually go more than that. Women usually go for older men."

Mitchell's heart sank another notch. Up until now, Carolyn's preference had been for older men—something he didn't need to be reminded of. He couldn't do anything about his age, so he'd been trying to win her heart in other ways, although all he could do was simply be himself, and he wasn't sure that was enough.

His mom finally appeared, and his dad left his side to help tuck his mom's jacket over her cast, then give her a small peck on the cheek.

"We'd better hurry. By now everyone's already at the house."

Mitchell gulped and swallowed hard. It was time.

æ

Carolyn smiled cordially at Gordie and Roland, who were the first to arrive. Fortunately, Jake and Ellen pulled in immediately after them, allowing her the chance to hide in the kitchen to wait for Mitchell. After that, she planned to stay only for as long as she needed to in order to be polite, then leave. She already had most of the food out and only needed to finish a few of the hot hors d'oeuvres. Then she would be free, and Mitchell could drive her home.

Silently, she kept busy doing things that didn't need to be done rather than standing around doing nothing while more and more people arrived. Just as she slipped on the oven mitts and was pulling the first tray of crab snaps out of the oven, she heard a female voice behind her.

"Miss Rutherford? Is that you? What are you doing here?"

The hot tray nearly dropped from her hands. She fumbled with it, letting it drop with a clatter to the top of the stove, and whirled around to see Melissa Roberts, one of her students from a few years ago, standing in the doorway, gaping at her.

She pulled the oven mitts off her hands and held them tightly. "I'm helping with the snacks, Melissa."

"I knew you were teaching night school, but I didn't know you were doing catering, too."

"Carolyn isn't here as the caterer, Melissa. She's here as my date."

The sound of Mitchell's voice nearly made her drop the oven mitts. Mitchell appeared behind Melissa, his face strangely pale, and his lips tightly drawn.

"Oh. Sorry." Melissa shrugged her shoulders and disappeared back into the living room, where the sound of laughter and conversation droned on.

Carolyn tried to force a smile and knew the effort fell flat. "You're the last one to get here. I was beginning to worry about you."

In the blink of an eye, Mitchell strode across the room until they were standing toe to toe. She would have backed up, except it would have sent her into the hot oven door, which was still open. He grinned, making his dimple appear. At the same time, the color returned to his face, and he rested his hands on her shoulders. "Did you miss me?"

"I wouldn't go that far."

It would have been impossible to miss him because even though he no longer lived in his parents' home, there were signs of Mitchell everywhere. She hadn't meant to snoop, but on her way into the kitchen after Mitchell and his parents left, she couldn't help but notice three eight-by-ten framed portraits prominently placed on the living room wall. One was his parents' wedding picture, with Kim and Roger in their wedding attire and a small child standing between them holding a ring bearer's silk pillow. Mitchell had been a beautiful three-year-old, and he'd grown into an equally handsome man.

The other two portraits were Mitchell's and Ellen's high school graduation pictures. Over the past six years, he hadn't changed all that much, except that time had matured his features.

After worrying about it, Carolyn had been relieved that Ellen hadn't been one of her former students, but Melissa had, and, of course, Melissa recognized her. She wondered if all the bridesmaids were former students.

She lowered her voice to a whisper to make sure no one suddenly appearing would hear. "Melissa was one of my students. What am I doing here?"

"You're here because you're with me. Don't worry about Melissa or any of Ellen's friends."

His hands moved from her shoulders to her cheeks. He lowered his head and kissed her gently, then dropped his hands and backed up.

The oven mitts she was holding landed on the floor. She quickly picked them up, brushed them off, and turned to close the oven door. "If I don't get those crab snaps out, they're going to be so cold, no one will be able to tell they're baked. You'll want to show them off when they're at their best."

Together, they began transferring the crab snaps to a platter.

"I don't think I'm going to tell anyone I've done all the food until most everything has been eaten. I want it to be a surprise. Besides, a few of the people here wouldn't touch anything if they knew I did the cooking."

"I think you're exaggerating."

"Unfortunately, I'm not. I'll go put these on the dining room table, and then I have to help Dad with something. I won't be gone long, but it might be a good idea to join Ellen's friends and just talk to them. You know, to bridge the gap. They're all in the working world now. I think it's just hard for them to think of you as anything besides their former teacher. You know, like teachers aren't people or allowed to have a social life outside the school. Unless you show them otherwise, they're going to keep thinking that way."

"I don't know. . . ."

He smiled and touched her shoulder, then lightly brushed one finger against her chin. "I'm serious. Show them the person you are outside of school."

Nervously, she glanced toward the doorway leading into the living room, as if by simply passing through it, things could be changed.

Most of her friends were her own age, but she thought of the people at her church, where the age gap was wide. There were women there who were in their mid to early twenties who addressed her by her first name, and to them, the age gap meant nothing because they had not previously known her. Likewise, she addressed ladies older than herself by twenty years or more by their first names, and the age gap meant nothing except more life experience. They were all equal in God's eyes as Christian sisters.

Again, she glanced to the doorway. "All right. I'll make the first move."

"Great. I'll catch you later when I'm finished with Dad." Mitchell picked up the tray and disappeared through the doorway, leaving her alone in the kitchen.

She didn't immediately follow him. First, she needed a few minutes to compose herself and work up her courage.

After multiple deep breaths, Carolyn ran her fingers through her hair, straightened her glasses, stiffened her back, and began the long journey into the living room.

Mitchell's older relatives sat on the couch and love seat, and the armchair remained empty. Ellen and the three bridesmaids stood in a small circle near the doorway, holding plates and nibbling at the goodies, totally engrossed in conversation. They didn't see her approach, giving Carolyn a chance to try to place them before she broke into their little circle.

She had never seen Ellen before, but Melissa had been in her homeroom a few years ago, and she recognized the other two as having attended her regular home economics class, but she couldn't remember their names.

Carolyn didn't want to eavesdrop, but her ears perked up when one of the girls leaned her head into the center of their little circle. "You won't believe this, but I saw Mitchell kissing Miss Rutherford!"

sixteen

Carolyn's feet skidded to a halt. Her heart pounded. She wasn't aware that anyone had seen what happened in the kitchen. Obviously, she and Mitchell were not as discreet as she had thought.

Melissa nodded her head. "I know. He said she was his date."

"Mitch? And Miss Rutherford?"

Carolyn heard a chorus of gasps. No one had seen her yet, but Carolyn feared if she moved, it would draw attention to her, and they would know that she had overheard. Her feet remained rooted to the floor.

All the heads stayed bowed in the small circle.

"He told me to call her Carolyn!"

"Get a life, Melissa. She does, like, have a name, you know."

"Yeah, but it feels so strange. She was my homeroom teacher. And now she's dating Ellen's brother."

"How old do you think she is?"

Carolyn watched the girls counting on their fingers and nodding. She wanted to yell out that she was only thirty-three, not ninety-three, and she had every right to date whomever she pleased, but she didn't want to make things worse.

She backed up a step, then froze when they lifted their heads, fearing they would notice her if she continued to move.

Melissa covered her mouth with her hands. "Ew. That would be like me dating Gordie's kid brother."

Carolyn's stomach clenched into a knot. Gordie's brother, Steven, was sixteen, in one of her classes, and at the moment he was hopefully getting over a crush on her.

All four of them gasped again, and Carolyn thought she

156

might throw up. She backed up another step until she was flat against the wall, but she couldn't get away.

The unnamed girl's voice rose a bit in volume, but she still continued to whisper. "You should have seen him kissing her. It was like in the movies. He was so romantic."

Melissa sighed. "Mitch can kiss me anytime!"

The girls giggled.

Carolyn no longer cared if they saw her. She turned and bolted into the kitchen. As she rounded the corner, she heard another round of giggles, telling her that her escape had been successful.

She drew in a ragged breath and slipped the last tray of crab snaps into the oven. This time, she would keep herself busy in the kitchen until Mitchell came back, regardless of his urging to let them get to know her as a person rather than a teacher. After hearing what Ellen's friends really thought, she couldn't face them alone. She wondered if she would be able to face them at all.

Just as she closed the oven door, Gordie and Roland appeared behind her. She wondered if they were ever apart.

Roland snitched a cheese ball from the tray on the table and popped it into his mouth. "Hi, Carolyn. I just wanted to say how great the food is. If I hadn't seen it for myself the other day, I wouldn't have believed Mitch did it. You helped him, didn't you?"

She turned and smiled at them, grateful for the distraction. "Except for the dessert, he made everything. I helped him a little, but not much."

"Mitch is a great guy, you know."

Her smile dropped. She had a bad feeling that Roland had come into the kitchen to talk to her about more than the food. She nodded and turned to check the last tray of crab snaps in the oven. "Yes, he is."

Roland swallowed a bacon-wrapped scallop, then cleared his throat. "Are you and Mitch, you know, going to continue seeing each other?"

She gritted her teeth at his question. She didn't know the answer. She had already committed herself to being Mitchell's date for the wedding, but tonight had shown her that it simply wasn't going to work. Mitchell had almost convinced her it was possible to keep seeing each other, but even his friends were questioning their relationship. She really didn't know what was right anymore.

At this point in her life, she was seeking marriage. Mitchell had completely shocked her when he told her that he loved her, not once, but twice. The first time she could have let it go, but after the second time, she couldn't help thinking that the natural progression would point toward marriage.

Mitchell was nothing like the man she had been praying for. Yet, despite everything, she wanted to keep seeing him, which was selfish and wrong.

The right thing to do would be to tell him she couldn't see him again, to tell him to find someone else to love, someone more suited to him—a woman he could be with, without being the subject of everyone's gossip.

She couldn't say anything like that to his friends. She had to say it to him in person.

"Yes," she answered, justifying her reply in her mind, knowing she hadn't been specific. "I'll be seeing him after tonight."

For a few minutes, they simply stood and stared at each other, making Carolyn feel like a bug under a microscope.

Gordie stepped forward, then fixed his gaze at some point on the wall behind her. "If you're wondering why we're asking, it's because Mitchell's been acting kind of funny. We haven't been seeing as much of him lately, and it's like when Jake started going out with Ellen, you know, seriously. We just wanted to know if you felt the same way."

Carolyn swallowed hard. Mitchell's quiet "I love you" echoed through her head, and her fingers immediately went to touch the little ring on the middle finger of her left hand—the little heart that said so much. It wasn't right, but she loved him, too.

"Yes," she whispered hoarsely. "I do feel the same way."

Gordie and Roland both nodded, then just as quickly as they arrived, they disappeared.

Carolyn's hands shook as she took the last tray of crab snaps out of the oven and set them on the counter to cool. She'd almost convinced herself to say good-bye to Mitchell, but the ache it brought to her heart was too painful. Using more concentration than needed for such a mundane task, she refilled the tray with goodies, leaving room for the last crab snaps, and told herself that now she had to stay put until they were cool enough to add to the tray.

While she waited, she tidied the kitchen until it was so perfect she had nothing else to do.

The time dragged. Laughter again drifted from the living room.

She stared out the window into the dark yard, where everything was quiet and still. Rather than joining the crowd or watching the crab snaps cool, she stepped out onto the large wooden patio deck, where the cool night air was pleasant after being close to the hot oven most of the evening. She leaned with her hands against the cedar railing beneath a large tree, which stood regally alongside the structure, and looked over the property.

Suddenly, footsteps tapped on the path that led through the yard.

Jake's voice split the silence of the evening. "So, what are you going to do?"

"I'm not sure," Mitchell mumbled. She could barely make out his words as they walked farther away. "I can't help feeling sorry for her. I'll have to think of something extra special. I know she likes cows."

Their voices faded as Jake and Mitchell disappeared around the side of the house. The gate squeaked open, then snapped shut.

Even though she still hadn't been able to figure out what it was Mitchell saw in her, she hadn't expected that he felt pity.

Immediately she thought of Killer, whom Mitchell had

taken home rather than allow the dog to be put to sleep. One of the reasons she'd been so quick to fall in love with him was his kind and compassionate nature.

She could understand why he felt sorry for her. She was more than aware of the pathetic creature she'd been when Mitchell had walked in to find her sunk to her knees in the middle of her living room floor, crying like a baby over the fiasco with Hank.

She suddenly realized that in the same way Mitchell felt so sorry for a poor, pathetic dog, that he gave it a good and loving home, he had declared his love to her—out of pity. She felt a sudden, almost physical, pain in her heart.

Before Mitchell came to find her outside and realized she'd overheard, she hustled back into the kitchen and started transferring the cooled crab snaps onto the tray.

Footsteps tapped on the linoleum floor behind her.

"What are you still doing in here?"

"Getting ready to put this out," she stammered, then cleared her throat. "Gordie and Roland were just here commenting on what a good job you've done with the food."

He glanced over his shoulder to the clamor coming from the living room. "They probably just came to snitch something while no one was watching." He faced forward and took one step toward her. "Never mind them. I came to pull you out of the kitchen. You've been spending too much time in here. You should join the party." He smiled wide and picked up one of the trays she'd finished preparing.

Her stomach tied into a knot, and she stepped closer to Mitchell so he couldn't see her trembling knees.

Their eyes met, steeling Carolyn's strength and nerve. She stood as tall as possible for someone barely over five feet tall and picked up a second tray of food. "Let's go."

She followed Mitchell into the living room, where everyone was engrossed in conversation.

Mitchell placed the tray on a table. In a flash, Gordie and Roland rose and headed for the food, causing everyone to groan.

Mitchell introduced Carolyn to everyone, then reached for her hand and held it, as if it were a normal occurrence. She did her best to hide her shock, but when Mitchell ran his thumb over the small ring, she completely lost track of everything that had been said and pretended to cough so she didn't have to respond.

When only a few tidbits remained on the tray, Ellen called for everyone's attention. "I want everyone to know that all this food you've just eaten and thought was made by Carolyn was actually made by Mitch. Except the dessert, right, Mitch?"

Carolyn thought she could have heard a pin drop.

Mitchell gave a carefree smile, but the tightness of his grip on her hand gave him away. Besides, the dimple wasn't showing. He didn't speak. All he did was nod.

Ellen waved her hands in the air. "Don't worry. No one is going to die. Carolyn taught him everything he needed to know, and I have it from a reliable source that even though she didn't actually prepare the food, she was there to supervise. Let's give them a big round of applause!"

Her cheeks grew hot at the response, but it gave her some relief to see that Mitchell blushed, as well.

Fortunately, since the wedding was tomorrow, the party wound down and guests began to leave. Mitchell saw them out, while Carolyn helped Kim pack up the leftovers.

"I don't know how to thank you, Carolyn, not only for your help, but for teaching Mitchell what to do in the kitchen. I've tried to get him interested for years and failed."

Carolyn smiled. "Believe me, it's nothing I said or did. He'd made up his mind before he signed up for the class. Like anything else, when you have to do something, you do what you can to get the job done."

"Yes, I can tell he's quite proud of himself." Silence hung in the air for a minute, then Kim spoke quietly. "How long have you and Mitchell been, uh, dating? He hasn't been to church or Bible study in quite awhile. I was starting to worry, and then I was told he's been going with you."

Carolyn snapped on the lids, and Kim tucked everything into the fridge. "We've been seeing each other quite frequently since he signed up for my cooking class."

"I guess what I'm trying to ask is if you're serious about him. He's my son, and I don't want to see him hurt. I also know that he'd be angry with me if he found out I've discussed this with you, but I had to ask. He hasn't seen much of us lately."

Carolyn forced herself to smile. "It's okay. You're not the first person to express concern."

Kim's face turned a dark shade of red, and she raised the uncasted hand to one cheek. "I'm so sorry! I don't know what to say!"

"It's okay, Kim. Or should I call you Mrs. Farris? It only shows how concerned everyone is about him. It's good to have such loving friends and family."

The red in Kim's face didn't change. "Please call me Kim."

All Carolyn could do was nod in agreement.

"I also hear you're coming to the wedding tomorrow as Mitchell's guest. I look forward to seeing you again."

Carolyn opened her mouth to speak, but Mitchell walked in before she could get a word out.

"You ladies finished? Or are you hiding in here because you're eating everything that's left?"

Kim smiled. "You did well, Mitchell. There's really very little left. Now if you two will excuse me, I'm off to bed. Tomorrow is a big day."

Carolyn picked up her purse and slung it over her shoulder.

Mitchell scooped up the bag of her empty containers. "Come on. I'll take you home."

She followed Mitchell to the car, and they made small talk all the way back to her house, where he left her at the door with a very sweet but chaste kiss.

She crawled off to bed, knowing she wouldn't be doing much sleeping.

Mitchell had told her that today, the day of the rehearsal, was the big day, but he was wrong.

Tomorrow was the big day. For the better part of the evening, she fully intended to enjoy every second she could with him because tomorrow she had to tell him of her decision—and stick with it.

Because after the wedding, she wasn't going to see him again.

෨

Carolyn studied herself in the mirror and tugged at the neckline of her snug dress. When she'd picked this dress specifically for Mitchell's sister's wedding, she only wanted to look good with Mitchell, who would be wearing a tuxedo, as would the rest of the men in the wedding party. She didn't know what had been running through her mind at the time, but her imagination and reality had suddenly collided, and it wasn't a pretty picture.

She sucked in her breath and turned sideways for one last view, then gave up and relaxed. The only person she was kidding was herself. She liked to eat and hated to exercise, which wasn't a great combination. She didn't know if it was realistic to hope for low lighting, but it was the only hope she had.

By the time the doorbell rang, she had nearly convinced herself to change. She ran her hands down her stomach one last time, sucked in her breath again, and walked to the door.

At the sight of Mitchell in a tux, her heart skipped a beat, then started racing. His neatly styled hair sported a fresh haircut and was gelled into perfect order, showing no trace of the orange and blue she'd spotted only yesterday when she sat beside him on the couch at his parents' house.

The cut of the suit emphasized the width of his shoulders and tapered down to his narrow waist, trim hips, and long legs. The cummerbund wrapped around his midriff for that finishing touch of potent appeal.

The pristine formal wear made Mitchell look older than his years, which was another perverse reminder of how young he was. Still, the suit also emphasized his handsome face and physique, and when he smiled, that adorable dimple appeared in his left cheek. The combination of the total package of

Mitchell Farris sent Carolyn's brain into a tailspin.

For lack of anything to say that wouldn't sound like a besotted teenager, she stood on her tiptoes and reached to straighten his slightly crooked bow tie.

He stiffened at her touch, which only confirmed her fears that she hadn't been seeing herself honestly in the mirror when she purchased the dress. To her surprise, when she wiggled his bow tie, his large hands settled on her hips. In a way, the contact helped to steady her but at the same time made her shaky inside.

She was in over her head. Way over her head.

Mitchell cleared his throat, then he reached up to touch the bow tie she'd just worked so hard to straighten. "You look great, Carolyn."

At his words, heat stained her cheeks. She sank to allow her heels to touch the floor, gave the bow tie a quick pat, and backed up a step. "You look great, yourself. I'm almost ready to go. I just have to get my shoes and a sweater in case it gets cool this evening."

She backed up another step to the closet, but instead of waiting outside, Mitchell also stepped inside and closed the door behind him.

"What are you doing? I thought we had to go."

His voice came out in a low growl. "This is going to be my last chance to kiss you today."

Before she knew what was happening, he'd backed her into the wall. He rested his hands on her shoulders, then used one index finger to tip up her chin, and their eyes locked. She knew what he was going to do, and she knew why he stopped. He was asking her permission.

All her hesitations crumbled. She was in love with him, right or wrong, and today was all they were going to have. All night long, she'd tossed and turned, trying to decide what to do. She had decided to enjoy the day with him, and then she was going to tell him it was over. This wasn't just her last chance to kiss him today. It was the last chance she would have to kiss him ever.

Carolyn closed her eyes and let her lips part just a little, and his mouth descended on hers.

This was not a sweet, chaste kiss. This time he kissed her like he meant it.

Carolyn melted against him. She slid her hands under the suit jacket and around his back and held him tight, then kissed him back in equal measure because she meant it, too. No one had ever kissed her like this before, and she knew no one ever would again.

When they separated, she could feel his reluctance as if it were a tangible thing. Slowly, he backed up, and his eyes fluttered open. "You're right," he ground out. "We had better go."

Carolyn continued to lean against the wall, needing the support.

Silently, they stared at each other. Mitchell's cheeks were flushed, his eyes were glazed, and his breathing was labored. She didn't want to think of what she looked like.

As they continued to stare at each other, they both started to smile.

Carolyn couldn't help herself. She actually giggled. "You're wearing lipstick." Another giggle escaped. "There's a man in a tuxedo in my house, wearing lipstick."

Mitchell smiled wider, but he didn't giggle. "That's really strange, because I'm looking at a beautiful woman all dressed up, who isn't wearing any."

She couldn't stop herself. Carolyn continued to giggle as she straightened herself, took one step toward Mitchell, grabbed him by the wrist, and pulled him into the bathroom.

Instead of being embarrassed, Mitchell pursed his lips at his reflection in the mirror, made a loud smooch in the air, then smiled at himself. "Mm-mmm, I do look good."

Carolyn handed him a tissue. "Quit fooling around. Wipe off the evidence. You have to be there early."

While he wiped the lipstick off, Carolyn reapplied hers, and they were soon ready to go.

She slid on her shoes and glanced at him one more time, and in so doing, she once again felt the heat in her cheeks. "Wait. You didn't get it all off. You're going to be in a lot of pictures today. I'd better do it."

They returned to the bathroom, where he sat on the edge of the bathtub while she diligently dabbed off the last smear.

The situation they were in could have been quite intimate, if they weren't in the bathroom and she didn't have a wad of lipstick-smudged tissue in her hand.

"There. You're manly once more. Let's get going, or you'll be late."

"Carolyn, wait. Before we go, there's something I almost forgot to tell you."

"Oh?" She smiled on the outside but cringed on the inside.

"I have to warn you; you'll really like Uncle Vince, but don't let him get started talking about fishing or you'll be sorry."

seventeen

Once at the church, Carolyn sat and watched the preamble to the wedding from a different perspective than at any other time she had attended a wedding. She watched Mitchell, Gordie, Roland, and even Jake run around checking on last-minute things.

"Mind if I sit with you for a while?"

Carolyn looked up to find Mitchell's father standing beside the pew.

"Of course not." She slid over to the side to make room for Roger, surprised that such an important figure in the coming proceedings would take time to say hello to her.

"The father of the bride isn't allowed with his daughter until she's ready to walk down the aisle. I guess I'm at loose ends. A little nervous, too, I don't mind saying."

Carolyn smiled. "It's an important day."

"Yes, it is. I think not only for my daughter."

Carolyn's stomach tied itself into knots. His expression told her he had something specific in mind.

Roger sat and turned sideways to face her. "I think I'm just going to be blunt, because I don't know how much time we'll have before I have to go. Mitchell seems to be very serious about you."

All Carolyn could do was nod.

"I know you have some concerns about Mitchell being younger than you are, and it doesn't help that Kim and I are not all that much older than you."

She nodded again. She couldn't believe she was having this conversation, today of all days, and with Mitchell's father—not that she'd done much talking.

Roger continued. "I don't know how much Mitchell has

told you about the start of Kim's and my relationship."

She cleared her throat, but her voice still came out far too unsteady. "I know you were both very young and were married when Mitchell was three."

He reached up and wiggled the knot of his tie. "That's right. We were young and stupid, and it was because of our age that we faced a lot of opposition, for a number of reasons. I know it's not quite the same for you and Mitchell, because Kim and I are the same age and we had each other." Suddenly, his ears turned red, making it apparent whom Mitchell got the trait from. "Kim is actually a few months older than I am. How about that, huh?"

She acknowledged that bit of information with a shaky smile, and he went on.

"All our friends were out having fun and letting their relationships mature the right way, before marriage, and especially before having children. Obviously we did it in the wrong order. Our parents helped, yet they didn't make it easy for us. We struggled and worked hard for a lot of years, even after we were married and managing on our own.

"When your kids are small, you tend to spend your time with people whose kids are the same age as your own. Because of that, we were ten years younger than the parents of Mitchell's friends, the people with whom we had the most in common and ended up spending most of our time with. We felt it then and we still do to a degree, but now that we're older, it doesn't make as much difference. I guess what I'm trying to say is that I know what it's like to face opposition and to struggle because something in your relationship is very different than the rest of your peers.

"Because we were so different than everyone in our circle, and because we made a lot of mistakes, Mitchell had to mature very fast for his years. Being so much older than all of his cousins and our friends' kids, he was the one to do all the baby-sitting and provide a good example. I wanted to ask you to give him a fair chance, based on Mitchell the person, not

Mitchell the younger man."

Roger's presence and heartfelt words only confirmed what she already knew. Mitchell was serious—too serious to think she could fool herself into being just friends. They could never be just friends. With Mitchell, it was all or nothing.

Roger was called away, and soon it was time for Jake and his groomsmen to stand at their places at the front of the church. Of course, Mitchell looked the best of all of them. As the bridal procession began, Carolyn watched Ellen's friends making their way to the front, but she couldn't help sneaking a peek at Mitchell when Ellen and their father began their march up the aisle. She could see the play of emotions running through him from pride to confusion, then something else she couldn't even begin to guess as he discreetly glanced from his sister to his best friend.

Even though she didn't know anyone well except for Mitchell, Carolyn found herself getting misty-eyed.

At the end of the touching ceremony, Carolyn stayed as much in the background as she could, standing silently by Mitchell's side as he chatted with other guests in the attached banquet hall.

She heard Mitchell's name being called in the background.

"Oops. I have to go to the park for the pictures now. Do you want to come?"

She shook her head. "It's okay. I see a few people I know from the school. It will be nice to talk to them."

He smiled, and Carolyn's foolish heart fluttered. "I'm glad you feel comfortable doing that. See you soon."

She walked with him to the church parking lot, where Mitchell slipped behind the wheel of Jake's vividly decorated car. As he drove the newlyweds to the park, he looked so happy that it made her regret what she would have to tell him at the end of the evening. Today was a wedding, a day to celebrate love. Despite what Roger had told her, it was not to celebrate hers and Mitchell's.

The guests mingled in every conceivable spot of the building, waiting for the wedding party to return. Carolyn recognized a few couples as former students or parents of present students. She strengthened her resolve and determined to see them as friends of the bride and groom. She was so successful that time passed quickly, and she was surprised when someone called out that Jake and Ellen had arrived.

Those who had not already found a table were quickly seated.

The speeches began, drawing everyone's attention to the front. Carolyn nearly cried at Mitchell's tender speech about his sister, then laughed at the way he expounded on Jake's not quite finest traits, and the entire group roared at his comments concerning his best friend marrying his sister.

After the toasts to the bride, Mitchell's pastor prayed, then the room buzzed with conversation and laughter as the meal was served. After the meal, there was a short video presentation of Jake and Ellen's childhood and courtship.

When the official program ended, the wedding party left the head table to socialize, starting with Jake and Ellen cutting the wedding cake and visiting with their guests.

Mitchell slid into the chair across from Carolyn.

As quickly as he had sat, he stood. "I don't want to sit here and call to you from across the table. Come on, let's go someplace else where we can talk without having to raise our voices."

Carolyn glanced from side to side. Small groups congregated everywhere, standing and sitting, and many people had already filtered into the lobby to talk where it wasn't so noisy.

She stood. "Sure."

≈

Mitchell led Carolyn out of the banquet room, through the nearly empty lobby, all the way outside. The sky was alive with the pink and purple hues of the sunset. The evening air was cool with the setting sun, and it was the perfect opportunity to wrap his arms around her, just to keep her warm because she'd left her sweater inside the banquet room.

"Mitchell?"

"I wanted to look at the sunset. It's kinda romantic, isn't it?"

"Romantic? It's the wedding getting to you."

"Maybe." He smiled and ran one finger over Carolyn's cheek. While he felt romantic, it had nothing to do with the beautiful sky or being at the uniting of two people before God. It was because he was with the woman he loved.

Despite the romantic atmosphere of the wedding and now the pretty sunset, all day long he'd had the nagging impression that something was wrong, but he couldn't put his finger on it. It had started long before the actual ceremony, when he arrived at Carolyn's house to pick her up. She'd been almost too responsive when they'd kissed earlier, like she knew something he didn't.

His stomach churned, despite his quickening heartbeat at the memory of a kiss that had rocked him to his soul. It was like the last kiss before the hero of the movie rode off into the sunset, never to be seen again.

Mitchell reached for her hand and twined their fingers together. This hero wasn't riding off into this sunset. He was staying, hopefully forever. Today, tonight, he was going to ask Carolyn if perhaps one day in the not too distant future, she would consider marrying him.

He wasn't going to rush her. After all, they hadn't known each other long, but all day he'd tried to squelch the panic he felt rising up, the fear that if he didn't do or say something right away, he was going to lose her.

"Listen! Do you hear the crickets chirping?"

He blinked, bringing his attention back to Carolyn beside him, which was what he had intended, not to go outside with her and be lost in his own little world. "There's a big piece of undeveloped land next door."

"Did you know that you can tell the temperature by a cricket's chirp? You count the number of chirps a cricket makes in fifteen seconds, and then add forty."

"That's very interesting. I never knew that." He almost started counting, but he stopped himself and squeezed his eyes shut. He wasn't there to learn about insect trivia. For weeks, he had waited for just that right moment to give her the promise ring, and it never happened. Then when he'd made his own moment after class, the wrong moment had turned exactly right.

Right moments didn't just happen, they were made, and he was going to make one right now.

He forced himself to relax, gave her hand a small squeeze, then turned and smiled at her. "Carolyn, I've been thinking. I know this is going to sound sudden to you, but will you—"

"Mitchell, wait."

Mitchell frowned. "Wait? But—"

"I know why you're doing this, and it's not necessary. You don't have to feel sorry for me."

"Sorry for you?"

"Because of Hank."

"But I—"

Suddenly, a voice called out. "Mitchell! Come on! Jake and Ellen are leaving."

"You have to go."

"No, we have to finish this."

"We can talk when everything is over. I have something to say to you, too."

❧

Once the last guest had left, Carolyn pitched in, and the cleanup progressed quickly. The mundane chores provided her the opportunity to be alone and allowed her time to think.

She could tell Mitchell knew what she was going to say to him. He wasn't his usual smiling self, and he was unusually quiet, while Gordie and Roland were unusually loud.

Also, his acquiescence meant that he had accepted what she was going to tell him.

To tell him she couldn't see him again was the most painful decision of her life. Over the last few days, she'd done a lot of thinking and even more praying, and she had concluded that Mitchell was not the man she'd been asking God for. She thought about all the qualities and criteria she asked for in the man who would be her husband, and of them all, Mitchell only met one—he was a Christian. She'd asked for God to show her whether Mitchell was right for her or not. For all her prayers, she hadn't seen anything that showed her Mitchell was the man God had chosen for her to share the rest of her life with.

Therefore, she had to quit fooling herself. A bad case of the warm fuzzies wasn't enough of a foundation on which to base a marriage. Something firm had to come first, something to help the relationship withstand the test of time. She'd had more reminders of everything wrong than the only thing right in their relationship, so she had to accept that as her answer.

There was no middle ground, because for this question, the answer was for keeps.

When the decorations were packed away, the room restored to its original order and properly cleaned, the wedding party left the building and walked to the parking lot.

Carolyn followed Mitchell to his car.

"Let's talk when you take me home. This isn't something I want to do in a moving vehicle," she said as he located his key ring and opened the door for her.

"Okay," Mitchell said quietly. He walked around to the driver's side and slid into the seat in silence.

She could tell that he had prepared himself for the worst, accepted it, and taken it like a man. A mature man.

She thought of what Hank had done when she turned him down. The older man, the one who seemed to be everything she'd ever wanted in the man who would be her mate. Mitchell rested one hand on the steering wheel and inserted the key in the ignition, but he didn't turn it. He sighed deeply, then dropped his hands and turned his body toward her. "We don't to have that little talk, Carolyn. It's okay. I know what you're going to say, and I won't insult you and keep hammering at you. Your decision is your decision, whether it's the one I want or not."

A burn started in the back of her eyes, but she blinked it back.

"I don't know if I'll have the strength to do this later, so I had better do it now." He reached behind the seat, pulled out a plastic bag, and handed it to her. "I got this for you. I forgot to give it to you before the wedding. You can ignore the note."

She opened the bag, reached inside, and pulled out a little plush ram that matched the sheep Mitchell had bought for her at the zoo. Stuck to it was a small note with Mitchell's scrawling handwriting.

> *To Carolyn.*
> *Husband attached.*
>   *Love, Mitchell*

She stared at the little ram, then at Mitchell.

He smiled weakly, like he was trying to lighten the heavy moment. "I hope this time you're not going to hit me over the head with it."

She petted the little ram, which was obviously the husband for the sheep now sitting on her bed, reread the note, and contemplated its message.

She swallowed hard. "Were you going to ask me if I wanted a husband, too?"

He smiled, but his face held no humor.

"Yes, I guess I was."

She stared blankly at the plush ram in her hands, then raised her head to look across the space between them and studied Mitchell.

He was no longer the neat and tidy package he had been in the afternoon. The jacket of the tuxedo was crinkled. His carnation was squashed and missing half its petals. He'd spilled something on his shirt, the bow tie was crooked, and his hair gel had given up its hold long ago. And contrary to the claims of Mitchell's hairstylist, she could still see some orange and blue at the roots.

Mitchell never put on airs, nor did he pretend to be something he was not. Mitchell was, just as his father said, simply the person he was. Regardless of his age, his job, his visions for the future, or anything else—or maybe it was the combination of them all—Mitchell was the man she was madly in love with and always would be.

When it came down to the bottom line, Mitchell was a man of faith and character.

Suddenly, Carolyn had to force herself to breathe. Of all the Bible reading she'd done since she'd met Mitchell, one verse, Isaiah 32:8, sprang to mind. "But the noble man makes noble plans, and by noble deeds he stands."

For all his plans and reasoning behind them, whether it had been his strategy to prepare the food for the wedding, to his ideas for fun places to take her—in spite of her best efforts to avoid him—to his intentions to court her or the times they had simply prayed together, he'd always done the right and noble thing.

She'd never met a man nobler than the fine Christian man in the disorderly tuxedo in front of her.

She had been praying for the wrong things, but God had sent her the right man anyway.

Knowing that he had planned tonight to ask her to marry him, her eyes clouded, but she blinked back the tears. Before she spoke, she plucked the little yellow note off the ram, reached past the space between the seats, and pressed it onto the center of his chest. "Then the answer is yes."

Mitchell reached up to brush his fingers across the "husband attached" sticker in the middle of his chest, stared down at it, then raised his head, meeting her gaze. His voice came out gravelly and low, like he was having trouble comprehending what she'd just agreed to. "That's great. I feel all choked up. I don't know what to say."

Carolyn had no intention of becoming tangled in a big kiss in the bucket seats of a car in the middle of his church's parking lot. Instead, she leaned over the stick shift and rested her palm on the note stuck to the center of his chest. Beneath her touch, his heart pounded.

"Just say, Baa—aa—aa."